The Skip Tracer

D.L. Bjorngjeld

Published by Dennis L. Bjorngjeld
Forest Lake, Minnesota

ISBN 978-0-9981110-2-5

Layout & Design by Todd Anderson

Printed in United States of America

Chapter One

Saul Berkowitz looked up from the file he was reading. He squeezed his eyes shut and rubbed the bridge of his nose, something that he did reflexively whenever he was frustrated or perplexed. "Tim," he called out.

Almost immediately, a young man appeared in his office doorway. "Yes sir?"

"Tim, would you call Sonny and tell him I'd like to see him in our office as soon as possible."

"Sonny?" Tim questioned.

Saul, owner of Midwest Bail Bonds, had just days ago hired him – Timothy Wallace – with plans of training him to be a top bail bondsman for his firm. Saul saw Tim as a sharp, ambitious, single twenty-three-year-old that he thought could handle the stress of the bail bond business.

"Sorry, I wasn't thinking" Saul said. "Sonny is a Fugitive Recovery Agent. He prefers the title 'Skip Tracer.' In truth," he said pausing and looking Tim in the eye, "Sonny's a Bounty Hunter. His card is tacked to the bulletin board. He's the best there is at finding a 'skip'... someone who hasn't shown up for their court date. Someone who's going to cost us thousands, maybe tens of thousands of dollars. Or, in this rare case," he said tapping his finger on the file he held, then looking back at Tim, "hundreds of thousands of dollars... if we don't find him in time."

"Yes sir," Tim said. "I'll call him right away."

Saul was about to tell Tim that he needn't call him "sir," as their office is much less formal than that. But, then again, he kind of liked the sound of it and the respect it showed. He decided to let it continue for a while. Maybe next week he'd tell him he could drop the sir.

"If he's in town, ask Sonny to come to our office ASAP. Otherwise ask him to call me."

"Yes sir," Tim said, heading toward the bulletin board.

Saul liked that. Liked Tim's show of respect and his eagerness to do anything thrown his way.

In a few minutes, Tim was back at Saul's office door. "Have you got a minute to speak with Sonny? I've got him on line three."

"Yes, thank you," Saul said, reaching for his phone and punching line three. "Sonny!" he said cheerfully.

"Saul..." Sonny replied. "How have you been old friend."

"Good! Life is good and business is good. What are you up to this week?"

"Well, I was just planning a little trip to St. Thomas Island with my dear friend. Why?"

"I need your help on a big one, Sonny. I'm on the hook for two hundred large with the court if we don't find this guy. Five weeks ago he was supposed to be in court at nine a.m. and I'm real nervous about the guy. He's a no show and there doesn't seem to be anyone with any idea where he might be. I really need your help."

There was a long silence. Finally Saul asked, "What do you think, Sonny? We have some time, but with every day that passes it's more likely he's farther away... and more likely I'll develop an ulcer. "

Again silence.

After a few more moments, Sonny said, "Yeah, I can do it. You've been good to me when I needed it, and that's too big a commission to pass up. I'll be in your office this afternoon to get the particulars."

"Thanks, Sonny. See you in a while." Saul hung up and smiled, feeling much better about his predicament.

It was three-thirty in the afternoon, when Harrison Lee Sawyer Jr. – better known as Sonny – walked into the offices of Midwest Bail Bonds. "Hi Deb," he said, smiling at the attractive receptionist. "How's things?"

"Things are great," she said, returning the smile. "How's your love life, Sonny?" she asked in a playful way.

"Sometimes good... sometimes very good," he replied with a shrug and a grin. "Is the man in his office?"

"Yup. Go ahead on back." She flicked a thumb over her shoulder, giving him the go-ahead..

Deb's large, antiquated desk faced the front door of the office and the huge, south-facing front windows. The desk seemed to overwhelm the small waiting area for clients. Behind her desk was a partial wall, made of opaque glass that was there to block the view of visitors to the rest of the desks occupied by bail bondsman and other office staff. Sonny stepped around her desk and the glass wall, and headed for Saul's office at the rear of the small building.

Six decades ago, this downtown building had been "Sammy's Place", a small, corner bar, which Saul's father, Aaron Berkowitz, purchased and remodeled into the new offices of Midwest Bail Bonds. Two decades ago, Aaron retired and placed their family business in Saul's capable hands. Saul had been very proud the day he moved into the "big office," that had been his dad's for forty years.

Sonny greeted the staff as he moved through the maze of desks and file cabinets toward the big office. As he got to Tim Wallace, he reached out his hand. "Since I don't recognize you, you must be the Tim I spoke to on the phone earlier."

"I am," Tim said. "Tim Wallace. Nice to meet you."

"You too," Sonny said, noticing the firm handshake. Then, pointing, he said, "Gotta go see the man."

Tim nodded and sat back down at his desk.

Sonny knocked hard on the frame of Saul's office door as he walked in. "Hey there, Mr. Berkowitz, got a minute for a drifter like me?"

"For you Mr. Sawyer," Saul replied, turning his chair to face him, "I've got all the time in the world. Sit down, relax," he said, waving him to a chair.

They caught up on things for a bit, then Sonny asked, "Who's this latest skip?"

"Lyle Novak. Here's a copy of our file Deb made for you." Saul reached out and handed it to him.

"Think he's a difficult one?" Sonny asked, as he started to peruse the file.

"Yeah, he's up on aggravated assault and robbery charges... and has had a couple of similar convictions before. So he's not gonna be one of the easy one that comes in willingly."

"In that case, I think I'll get Dillon to help me with this one. See if we can get this guy back here in a few days for you, and I can get back to planning my trip to St. Thomas. My friend was a little miffed when I told her we may have to delay it a week or two. But she'll get over it."

"Yeah, this is probably a good one to have Dillon's help," Saul said. "Might get physical. I was going to try and talk you down from your nineteen percent on the risky ones but, since you gotta pay Dillon, I won't niggle you."

"That's good. I figured that discussion would be coming... glad we won't have to debate it. Is there still an empty desk in the corner that I can use for a little while this afternoon?"

"Yup, use it whenever you need. And good hunting, Sonny," Saul said, spinning in his chair back to his desk.

Sonny closed the file and walked out of Saul's office. He headed for the empty desk in the far corner of the main office and dropped the file on it. Pulling his cell phone from his pocket, he sat down on an old, rickety desk chair that barely held him up.

He brought up the Contacts file on his phone and scrolled to Dillon Bishop. He pressed the little telephone icon, and soon Dillon's phone was ringing. It rang three times, then he heard the familiar voice.

"Hey, Big Guy, how've you been?" Dillon asked.

"Been good... except that I haven't seen your smiling face in nearly a month."

"Make that a month and a half," Dillon said.

"Has it really been that long?" Sonny asked.

"Since we hauled in that Wyndowski character."

"Yeah, guess you're right. Time slips away... too fast. Got a minute to talk?"

"Sure. What's up?"

"I'm at Saul Berkowitz's office. He's got a big one that needs tracking and it's a big payday for us. Interested?"

"I am," Dillon said without hesitating. "It's really good timing, too... cause I'm in need of a payday. What'cha got?"

"I just started looking at the file, but Saul says the skip's got aggravated assault and a few other things, so it might get serious. Maybe a little rough 'n tumble."

"You and I have handled more than a few of those for Saul in our four years together. Got much on this guy?"

"Well, I just sat down with his file. I'm gonna dig through it this afternoon to see if anything jumps out as a place to start."

"When do you want to meet?" Dillon asked.

"My place, nine o'clock tomorrow morning?"

"I'll be there. Have the coffee on."

Chapter Two

"To expect bad men not to do wrong is madness."
Marcus Aurelius (121 – 180 AD)

The next morning, Dillon was at Sonny's door ten minutes early, as usual. Sonny had never known him to be late. Rather, Dillon liked to be at least ten minutes early for any appointment.

Sonny's home is in the Audubon Park area of Northeast Minneapolis. It's a very nice, quiet neighborhood of older homes, built mostly in the early twentieth century. His is a small, Tudor style home that's very nice and very clean. Mostly thanks to Caitlin, the woman who gives it a good cleaning on the first Monday of each month.

Dillon rang the doorbell and heard Sonny shout, "Come on in, Dillon."

He let himself in and found Sonny sitting at the table finishing his breakfast. After a few pleasantries and getting himself a fresh cup of coffee, Dillon asked, "Have you got anything on this guy yet?"

"Well... a little... maybe."

"A little... maybe? Oh boy, that narrows it right down," Dillon said, with his usual sarcasm.

"Actually, I spoke with a couple of this guy's relatives yesterday, and it seems his Grampa was the only one he was ever close to. Gramps has a place along the river in Clearwater. I think that's as good a place as any to start looking. Did you bring your gear with you?"

"Got it all in my trunk. I was hoping you would say we could get started this morning. Let's hit the road, Big Guy."

Earlier, eating breakfast, Sonny was thinking about the comment Dillon had made yesterday afternoon on the phone – that they'd brought in more than a few rough characters in the past four years. It was no small thanks to Dillon's toughness and fearlessness.

Dillon Bishop is six-one, and a solid two hundred-twenty pounds. He grew up in Northeast Minneapolis and was involved in Golden Gloves boxing for several years, then later in MMA fighting. He gave it up when he figured out that, no matter how tough you are, there's always another guy coming up that's tougher than you.

The decision to move on became much easier when Sonny offered Dillon a chance to work with him in the Skip Tracing business, and explained the kind of money he could make. Dillon always respected Sonny, and called him "Big Guy," even though Sonny is only two inches taller and twenty pounds heavier.

The two had become close during the four years they worked together, though they seldom socialized together. Maybe because of their age – Dillon is twenty-four and Sonny thirty-eight. But when they worked together, they were as close as two men could possibly be.

They loaded Dillon's gear into the back of Sonny's black Tahoe and headed up Interstate 94 toward Clearwater. As they traveled, Dillon read through the file trying to see if there was anything Sonny might have missed. "Looks like Grampa's place is on Falcon Circle, just north of downtown Clearwater," he said, closing the file. "How do you think we should go at this?"

Sonny glanced at Dillon, saying, "What would you think about using our Census Bureau thing?"

"Well, Gramps or Novak might know that they only do the census every decade, meaning the next one wouldn't be until 2020."

"Remember how we used it in 2015, telling folks Minnesota updates every five years. We can probably come up with some lame excuse that most people won't even question when they see our official looking jackets and signs on the Tahoe."

"Yeah, you're probably right," Dillon said. "All we need is enough time to get in Grampa's door and for you to ask to use the bathroom so you can snoop around a bit, while I keep him busy in the kitchen. The big magnetic signs on the Tahoe and our official looking jackets will probably buy us that little bit of time."

At Clearwater, they cruised up County Road 75 and found Falcon Circle. They turned onto the Circle, then stopped and parked the Tahoe on the side of the street, about six houses away from Grampa's place. Then, with each taking one side of the street, they knocked on doors and spoke with homeowners, asking them the questions they had made up on their official looking forms. This was done to allay any fears Grampa or Lyle Novak might have, in case they were closely watching the neighborhood for anything, or anybody, that was out of place or unusual.

Soon, they came to the home of Mr. Joseph Kramer, Lyle Novak's Grampa on his mom's side. Dillon walked up the sidewalk to the front door, while Sonny parked the Tahoe in front of the next house past Grampa's. So far, neither of them had seen any movement in the Kramer house.

Dillon rang the doorbell, looking down at the clipboard that held the fake forms. A gentleman, one that Dillon guessed to be nearing seventy years old, opened the door saying, "Can I help you?"

"Yes sir, we are updating information on residents we were unable to contact during the previous census. Would you mind if I came in and asked you a few questions that are very general and shouldn't take more than a couple minutes of your time."

"And, would you mind," Sonny shouted, hurrying up the sidewalk, "if I use your bathroom for a moment. I just moved our vehicle and have a really urgent need."

"I guess so," the man said. "Come in." He pushed the door open and stepped aside to let the two in.

Sonny said, "Thank you so much. I don't know what I would've done." He raised his hands, palms up, and repeated, "I just don't know what I would have done."

Laying it on a little thick, Sonny, Dillon thought.

They sat at the kitchen table and Dillon began asking Mr. Kramer the questions on their forms. He spoke loudly, trying to make cover for Sonny, and any noise he might make while quickly snooping around.

After a few minutes, Dillon said, "Well, that's it. We'll get out of your hair." He heard Sonny on the other side of the wall between the kitchen and the hallway, and figured he might open the garage door to sneak a peek, so he repeated – maybe a little too loudly – "Thank you, again, for being so cooperative," and reached to shake Kramer's hand. "I wish everyone was as friendly and cooperative as you."

Mr. Kramer smiled a bit, and said, "Glad to help. Good luck with the rest of your surveying."

Dillon, hearing the quiet click of the garage door closing, quickly fumbled his clipboard to the floor, trying to distract Kramer. Picking it up, he brushed it off and gave Kramer an embarrassed smile, hoping to disarm him if he was at all suspicious.

Acting a little "buffoon-ish" was something Dillon had picked up from watching Sonny. It let a person, particularly a suspect, feel more at ease in dealing with "this moron." Most of the time it would disarm the person to the point of sheer surprise, when Sonny morphed into the "enforcer."

"Ready to go, partner?" Dillon shouted.

"Sure am," Sonny said, as he stepped around the corner, reaching toward Mr. Kramer to shake his hand. "Thank you so much. You saved me. We'll be on our way. I hope the rest of your neighbors are as pleasant and helpful as you've been."

After knocking on a few more doors, talking to a few more neighbors, and moving the vehicle a couple more times, in case they were watching from the Kramer house, they ended their "survey."

"Well? Did you find anything good at Kramer's?" Dillon asked.

"Yeah, I did. Lyle Novak has a red, 2008, Chevy Trailblazer, license number 396 PRK. It's in the garage, so he's either in a room in the basement or not there right now."

"Really? That's about as good a start as we could hope for on one like this."

"It is," Sonny said. "Now, we just have to figure out where we can set up surveillance and watch for Novak."

"How 'bout we find a place for supper and talk about that dilemma over a plate of food."

Sonny turned the Tahoe around, drove back through the neighborhood to scout the possibilities, then headed for downtown Clearwater to find a restaurant.

Chapter Three

"Death smiles at us all; all we can do is smile back."
Marcus Aurelius (121 – 180 AD)

They ordered dinner at the Silver Kettle. Waiting for their food, Sonny said, "Surveillance from the house across the street would be best, obviously. We could explain to the widowed woman there, that Lyle Novak is a wanted fugitive and may be endangering his grandfather, Mr. Kramer."

"Sounds good," Dillon said. "I can't believe it would take more than a day. He's gotta move around sometime."

After dinner they had drinks at Brad's Bar across from the Silver Kettle, then drove to a motel they'd noticed when exiting the Interstate. They got a room with two queen beds and settled in for a good night's sleep. From experience, they knew they wouldn't likely be getting any good sleep for the next couple of days.

In the morning they visited the Silver Kettle again, had breakfast, then drove out to speak with the woman in the home across from Kramer. They wore their jackets with "Fugitive Recovery Agent" and showed her their impressive identification. She was a very friendly woman who cordially invited them in. They sat at her small kitchen table, carefully explaining about the surveillance they would like to do from her home – trying to find Lyle Novak and protect Mr. Kramer. The lady, Mrs. May Wagner, was eager to be of help in protecting Mr. Kramer from any danger or legal trouble. "You're welcome to use my home for as long as you need. Pull your vehicle into the garage as well. It's empty, except for my little car."

"We'll do that and, if you don't mind, we'll set up a telescope and camera behind your sheer curtains in the living room to watch Mr. Kramer's home," Sonny said. "It's so nice of you to offer so much help. We will be out of your hair in a day, two at the most, Mrs. Wagner."

"I don't mind a bit, and you'll stay as long as you need," she said. "And, please, call me May. You've had breakfast already, so I'll plan on making us some ham and cheese sandwiches for lunch, if that's okay."

"We'd love that," Dillon told her.

Sonny pulled his Tahoe into her garage, closed the garage door and got the telescope and camera from the back of his vehicle. Dillon set them up in the living room, aiming them at Kramer's kitchen window.

Now they would start the long, boring, tedious task of watching for Lyle Novak. If and when they caught sight of him, they'd immediately move to apprehend him – hopefully without any major confrontation.

The morning hours passed quickly. One of them had to keep a watchful eye on the telescope at all times, so not to miss any chance of spotting Novak. They relieved each other every half hour.

It was a little after twelve, and Mrs. Wagner was in her kitchen preparing sandwiches. In a few minutes, she announced, "Lunch is ready, gentlemen. Come whenever you're ready."

Dillon said. "I'll go eat lunch now and be back to relieve you, so you can go have yours."

Sonny nodded. "Works for me."

After watching the Kramer house for more than a day and a half, both Dillon and Sonny were beginning to wonder if Novak was actually there. Finally, Sonny looked up from the telescope, stood up from his chair, stretched and said, "I gotta think we'd have at least caught a glimpse of Novak moving around by now."

"Yeah, if he is there," Dillon said, "you'd think he'd visit Gramps in the kitchen once in a while, since that's where Gramps spends most of the day watching TV and playing on his computer. Or Gramps would go downstairs to visit him sometime. I think it's time we go knock on the door again and check things out."

"I agree," Sonny said.

"Give me a few minutes to get to the back side of the house in case he's there and tries to run," Dillon said.

They both checked their side arms to be sure they were fully loaded, and jacked a cartridge into the chamber. "Take the M11 with you," Sonny said, "since it's more likely he'd try to bolt out the back."

The M11 is a less lethal firearm that shoots rubber bullets designed to knock down and, hopefully, incapacitate a suspect for a short while. Sonny had recently purchased the Defenzia M11 and really liked the way it handled. Much better than the old "Papa Thorson" beanbag gun he'd used for years. The M11 also fires a "Flash-Bang" round that will blind suspects for as much as a minute.

Sonny waited in May's house for a few minutes, to give Dillon time to circle around back. While he waited, he explained to May what they were doing. "Hopefully, if he's in there, he'll come without trouble."

"You be careful," May said.

"We sure will," Sonny said with a quick nod and smile.

He stepped out her front door, crossed the street and hurried up the sidewalk to Kramer's front door. He paused a moment, breathing slowly and calming himself, then rang the doorbell and tapped on the door.

Joe Kramer opened it and, recognizing Sonny, smiled and asked, "How can I help you this time?"

"Mr. Kramer," Sonny said, trying to be as polite as he could be, "is your grandson, Lyle Novak, here with you?"

"No, he's not. Why do you ask?"

"Well, when I and my partner were here the other day, I noticed his red Trailblazer was in your garage. How is it that his vehicle is here and he's not?"

"Well, you should have asked," Kramer said. "I could have explained it to you. I had a 2004 Chevy Silverado pickup that he wanted. Said he needed it to haul stuff for his work. I figured they were about the same value. Mine is a bigger, more expensive vehicle, his is a newer one, so we traded even up. I've had the Trailblazer for a few days now and love it."

Sonny took a notebook from his shirt pocket and began writing notes. "What color is the Silverado?"

"Dark green."

"Do you remember the license number?"

"Yeah, 974 WNP. Why are you asking about all this? And about my grandson?"

"Your Grandson was released on bail and didn't show for his court date. My partner and I are Fugitive Recovery Agents and have been hired by Midwest Bail Bonds to bring him back for his court appearance."

Mr. Kramer stared at Sonny for a long moment, then finally said with a bit of disdain in his voice, "You're Bounty Hunters."

"Yes sir, we are," Sonny said, matter-of-factly.

He was never apologetic for being a bounty hunter. He preferred the title "Skip Tracer," but was not offended by Bounty Hunter, Bail Enforcement Agent, Fugitive Recovery Agent, Bail Recovery Specialist, or any other euphemistic title people used to describe his profession.

He saw what he did as necessary to society's well-being. Just as policemen were there to enforce our laws and arrest any person who would break them, he saw what he did as part of the overall justice system.

The number of lawbreakers – alleged lawbreakers – that were out on bail waiting for a court appearance and did not show up for their hearing absolutely astounded him. When he first looked into the profession of bounty hunting, he interviewed several bail bondsmen and was told the number of "skips" across the United States at any given time is in the thousands.

With his military background – ten years in the United States Army's 75th Ranger Regiment – his size and physical condition, he was encouraged by all of the bondsmen he spoke with to join the ranks of bounty hunters. Like the United States Marines, bail bondsmen were always "looking for a few good men."

19

During his time with the U.S. Army, he had two deployments in Iraq and one in Afghanistan. When he retired from the Army, he thought he'd be going to accounting school, with ambitions to become a CPA. After a month and a half in school, he knew the accounting profession wasn't for him.

By sheer coincidence, he met Saul Berkowitz having a late dinner one evening at the Shaw's in Northeast Minneapolis. The burgers and fries at Shaw's are Sonny's favorite. And, evidently, were Saul's as well. They struck up a conversation, which eventually came around to the subject of bounty hunting.

Saul liked Sonny's physical size, self-confidence and his military background. He suggested Sonny do a couple ride-alongs and captures with one of Saul's better bounty hunters. "That's the best way to learn the trade... and see if it suits you. Here's my card. Give me a call if you'd like to try it sometime. I think you'd be very successful at it."

Chapter Four

"Live life with truth and justice, tolerant
those who are neither true nor just."
Marcus Aurelius (121 – 180 AD)

Later, headed back to Minneapolis, Sonny said, "I think Novak's idea of trading vehicles was to make it harder to track him, not to haul anything for work... he doesn't have a job. But, I guess it bought him a couple extra days already, and that really chaps my hide."

"Hey, not a big loss," Dillon said. "What next?"

"Give Saul a call and ask him to get the phone records for Joe Kramer, and anything else that he can on him."

"Sure," Dillon said, pulling his phone from his pocket and punching up Saul's number. "What'cha thinkin'?"

"Well, we don't have a working number for Novak, so he might have picked up a throw-away. Maybe Kramer's phone bill will show a number that we can't trace back to anyone. It may give us...."

Dillon held up a finger interrupting Sonny. "Hi Deb, it's Dillon. Can I speak to Saul... thanks Deb."

He nodded toward Sonny to let him know she was connecting him. "Hello Saul, this is Dillon."

Saul asked how it was going. "Well, we had two good days of surveillance on Novak's Grampa – Joe Kramer, who had Novak's car in his garage – but we came up empty. We're wondering if you could get Kramer's phone records. Sonny thinks it might give us a lead to Novak's whereabouts."

"Sounds great, Saul," Dillon said. "We'll be in your office later this afternoon."

At four o'clock that afternoon, Sonny and Dillon were in the receptionist area of Midwest Bail Bonds, flirting and having fun with Deb as they usually did. Sonny leaned his head to the side to see around the glass wall and saw Saul standing in his office doorway, hands held out to the side and a look that said, "Are you coming back here or what?"

"We better git. The Man is waitin' for us," Sonny said, grabbing Dillon by the elbow.

Then seeing them coming, Saul turned and said loudly, "Chris, got anything on Kramer's phone yet?"

"Just printing it right now, boss. Be there in a minute." Chris shouted. Chris Savage was the closest thing to a tech expert that Saul had ever had at Midwest Bail Bonds – and he was good, really good. He amazed everyone in the office with his ability to get just about anything they needed through regular sites, as well as hacking into private systems they wanted to get information from.

Sonny and Dillon walked into Saul's office and Saul pointed at two empty chairs, inviting them to sit. "It's been a while, Dillon," Saul said. "How've you been?"

"Been great, Saul. Anxious to get back to work for you, so I was happy to hear from Sonny."

Just then Chris walked in, handing out copies of several pages of Kramer's latest phone bills, and a copy of a land deed that was in Kramer's name. "Thanks, Chris," Saul said, looking up from the papers.

Chris nodded, and returned to his desk.

Saul's office was quiet for a couple minutes as they scanned the information Chris had provided. "I think we got what you're looking for," Saul said, looking up from the papers he held.

Sonny smiled at him, saying, "Tell me... I don't see it yet."

"Kramer has a hundred and twenty acre piece he owns near Palisade, Minnesota. That's a copy of the deed you have. There are two calls on Kramer's latest phone bill that originated from that area last week. I'm bettin' that's where Novak is... or was. And, I'm bettin', that's the phone number for a throw-away he bought."

"You've still got it Saul... that special sense to sniff things out," Sonny said, smiling again. "Think Chris could put a tracer on that phone... that throw-away?"

"Don't know. But we can find out in a hurry." Saul called out, loudly, "Chris."

Soon, Chris was at the door asking, "What's up?"

"This phone number I've circled, can you put a trace on it and find out where it's at?" Saul asked, holding the paper toward Chris.

Chris took the paper and glanced at it. "Sure can," he said. Then he hesitated for a moment, looked up from the paper and said, "I shouldn't say that so quickly. If he's on the run, he may turn it off and pull the SIM card, so he can't be traced. But if it's on or he uses it again, I can pick it up and locate him in no time at all."

"Okay, let's get on it Chris," Saul said. "If you pick up anything, let Sonny know immediately."

"Got it," Chris said, nodding toward Sonny as he turned and headed back to his desk.

"If I remember right," Sonny said, "Palisade is nearly a three hour drive from here. So, rather than search unfamiliar territory in the dark, I think we'll drive to Aitkin and stay in a motel. Then we can talk to the Aitkin County Sheriff's office in the morning, and we're only a half hour from Palisade."

"Let's hope you find him," Saul said. "With any luck he's holed-up there for a while."

Chapter Five

"When you arise in the morning think of what a privilege it is to be alive."
Marcus Aurelius (121 – 180 AD)

They had an early breakfast at the Birchwood Café in Aitkin. Sonny drank the last of his coffee, and said, "Let's go see who's on duty at the Sheriff's office this morning."

After explaining to a Deputy Sheriff the reason for their business in Aitkin County, they headed north out of Aitkin on Hwy. 169. They found the Great River Road that follows the Mississippi River – and isn't such a great road – east toward Palisade. Kramer's land was wooded and ran along the south side of the road at about 330th Ave., with only a small trail leading to a shack tucked back in the woods.

Just beyond where they found a trail that headed off into the woods, hopefully to Kramer's shack, they found a spot to park their vehicle off the road. Closing the doors quietly, they each checked their side-arm. From the back of the vehicle, Sonny grabbed a Taser and Dillon grabbed the M11. Then they eased the rear door shut.

"You take this side. Stay in the trees about thirty yards away from the trail. I'll cross over and stay about thirty yards on the other side," Sonny said.

Dillon nodded and slowly started in, looking for the shack. Sonny crossed the trail and kept Dillon in sight. They moved slowly and quietly. Soon, Dillon could see a small shack down the slope and wondered if Sonny could see it. When Sonny glanced his way, Dillon pointed. Sonny nodded and indicated to keep moving ahead slowly.

Suddenly, a rifle shot rang out and the bullet caught the edge of a tree above Dillon's head, spraying chunks of bark down on him. Both men dropped to the ground.

"Hold it right there," a voice shouted from inside the shack. "You obviously don't know that this is private land. I don't want to shoot you, but I will if you don't turn around and get on outta here."

"You sure you want to do that?" Sonny shouted.

Immediately, there was another rifle shot that caught the edge of a tree above him and sprayed bark down on him. *That answers that*, Sonny thought, as he hugged the ground. *Seems to be a pretty good shot with that rifle, too.*

Sonny rose to his hands and knees, motioning for Dillon to retreat to the vehicle. Both men hurried, jogging back to the Tahoe.

"That guy's a pretty good shot," Dillon said. "Trying to be cute and spray us both with some tree bark."

"Yeah," Sonny sighed. "He's gotta have a motion detector system to pick us up that far from out the cabin. We're gonna have to figure that out. First though, let's circle wide and see if he's got a "back door" way out of this place. Meet you on the far side."

Dillon headed out, slowly circling wide left of the shack. Sonny circled wide in the other direction. Neither one knew what they were looking for exactly, but anything out of the ordinary would tell them if Novak had another way to get out of this place. Sonny couldn't imagine him staying here if he didn't have one.

As Sonny circled toward the rear of the shack, he crossed a small trail that looked like it had been lightly used by a four-wheeler. He stood on the trail and looked both directions. *That's as good a way as any*, he thought, *to sneak away from trouble.*

He continued to circle until he could see Dillon coming from the other direction. He stopped, waved and waited for him to get there. "I think I found his escape route. A four-wheel trail headed southeast from the shack."

"I didn't see any motion detectors, or anything else unusual," Dillon said. "He must have them planted closer to the shack."

"That's the next puzzle we have to solve," Sonny said, removing his cap and scratching his head. "Let's go back this way so I can show you the trail," he said, pointing with his cap, then replacing it on his head.

They circled back and found the trail that zig-zagged through the trees, then out across an open, wet, low area. "Looks like it goes across the wet area and past that big tree on the other side, as it climbs up out of the low area. That huge oak looks like a good place for you to hide and wait for him. Now that he knows where here, he may try to bolt on us at any time. I didn't see his pickup, so he must have it stashed at the other end of this trail.

"Why don't you head over and get comfortable behind that tree. I'll go get you your pack, water, and anything else I think you'll need for a stakeout and bring it out to you. You may have to be there for a while, waiting and watching for him. I'm going to somehow shut down his motion detector system. Then, after I let him stew a while, I'll start to move in on him."

"Grab that five gallon bucket with the padded cover," Dillon said. "That'll give me something comfortable to sit on and, if need be, it works great as a porta-potty with the plastic bags and TP inside."

"Be back with it all in about twenty, twenty-five minutes," Sonny said, turning and heading toward their vehicle at a fast pace.

As he circled back toward the Tahoe, he wondered how he would foil Novak's motion detector system. He finally decided that he'd just locate a couple of the sensors and disarm them. Then he'd let Novak sit nervously for a while in the shack. With his system down, he'd have to decide to either stand his ground and fight, or book it on the four-wheeler. Either way, Sonny knew they would get him... hopefully without serious injury to anyone.

From the back of the Tahoe, he grabbed Dillon's backpack which was filled with food, snacks, bottles of water, binoculars and other small equipment needed for a long stakeout. He reached for his Mossberg 500 shotgun – a 20 gauge, equipped with a pistol grip and an 18 ½" barrel. He added a box of twenty 3" shells to the backpack. Carrying the pack, shotgun and pail, Sonny headed back toward Dillon at a fast pace.

Reaching the trail, he turned and followed it across the low wet area and up a slight rise to the huge oak tree. As he neared, Dillon stepped out from behind the tree. "Good," he said as Sonny neared. "I forgot to mention the shotgun, but I see you've got it."

"Yeah, I think there's enough here for a good twenty-four hour stakeout... if need be," Sonny said, setting the equipment behind the tree.

"Got a plan yet, for what you're going to do up front?" Dillon asked, as he knelt to take things from his pack.

"Yeah, not much of one. Think I'm just gonna find his motion sensors, break them, and let him wonder who we are for a little while. I'll keep you updated with the radio. Is yours tuned to channel eleven?"

Dillon reached in one of the outside pouches on his pack and took out the radio. He turned it on, heard a loud static noise and adjusted the squelch until the noise disappeared. "Yup, we're on channel eleven."

Sonny did the same with his radio, then pressed the talk switch and said, "Check... check." He heard it come through Dillon's radio and nodded. "Good to go. I'll be back to you in a while."

As Sonny turned to leave, he thought of saying something about their need to take Novak alive, but knew Dillon was well aware of this and didn't need reminding. He decided to start at the front and slowly work his way in, since that's where Novak's system had first picked them up.

From the Tahoe he moved slowly, zig-zagging his way toward the shack, watching for surveillance equipment of any kind. Finally, ahead to his left, he saw what looked like a motion sensor nailed to a tree. His eyes followed the line to the right, until he finally saw another sensor mounted on a 2"x 4" post between two small trees. He eased his way toward the one on the post between the two small trees.

As he reached it, he paused for a moment studying the sensors and the shack. He couldn't think of a better way to solve the problem, so he raised his boot, kicked the post over and stomped the sensor into the leaves and dirt.

There were three small windows in the shack, and he could see Novak's silhouette hurrying from one to another. Finally, he shouted from inside, "Guess you boys made your choice. Decided to test me, huh? Big mistake."

Sonny keyed up his radio and quietly spoke. "You there Dillon?"

"Go ahead."

"I disabled his motion system. Now he's threatening to kill us. Think I'm going to stay put for a while. Keep a good eye out, he may decide to bolt rather than fight us."

"Roger that."

Sonny removed his pack, dropped it to the ground and sat down on a large fallen log. He had two large trees between him and the shack for cover, and could lean left or right and have a good view of the shack and the surrounding area. He brought out a snack bar and bottle of water from his pack, and got ready to relax for a while.

After about forty-five minutes, Sonny heard what he thought sounded like a four-wheeler's engine starting. If it was, it was the quietest one he'd ever heard. He grabbed his radio, "Dillon, I think I hear a four-wheeler. Be ready."

"I'll be ready," Dillon whispered, as he reached for the M11, checking to be sure it was loaded and ready.

Soon, Sonny was sure it was a four-wheeler, as the engine noise grew louder. He got to his feet and moved to the side until he caught a glimpse of Novak riding away.

He grabbed the radio again, and said, "He's headed down the trail toward you."

"I can hear him now. I'll be ready," Dillon said.

Sonny began jogging after Novak, trying to keep him in sight, yet not be seen by him.

Dillon thought about the Defensia M11. At the gun range it was accurate to about forty yards, but he decided to wait until Novak was climbing the short slope out of the wet area. At that point, he would only be about fifteen yards away when Dillon stepped from behind the tree. He had the shotgun leaning against the tree, ready to grab if he failed with the M11. With the shotgun, he'd have to shoot low and take a leg out to keep Novak alive.

He heard the engine of the four-wheeler getting louder and peeked around the tree. He could see Novak coming at a pretty good pace, weaving through the trees toward the low, wet area. Now he would have to wait and judge – by the sound of the engine – when Novak was climbing out of the wet area and nearing the tree.

He huddled behind the tree, his anxiety level getting higher by the second. As the four-wheeler came closer, he heard the engine accelerate a little as though climbing the slope out of the wet area. He stepped from behind the tree, aimed center mass on Novak and fired.

He hit Novak squarely in the chest and toppled him from the four-wheeler, which then lurched to the left and ran into a birch tree. As advertised, the M11 stunned Novak, giving Dillon enough time to be on him, roll him over and handcuff his wrists.

As Dillon got to his feet, Novak was cussing loudly. "Quiet," Dillon shouted, "or I'll thump you in the back of the head with that shotgun and put you're lights out for a while."

He reached for his radio, thumbed the key and said, "C'mon in, Sonny. Novak's cuffed."

"Way to go partner!" he heard back on the radio.

Clipping the radio on his belt, he walked over to the four-wheeler. The engine was still running, so he reached for the key to shut it off, then hesitated. Instead, he hopped on, shifted it into reverse and backed it away from the birch tree. Then he turned it around and shut the engine off. He glanced across the wet area and saw Sonny coming through the large trees at a fast pace, then he glared down at Novak.

Chapter Six

"The soul becomes dyed with the color of your thoughts."
Marcus Aurelius (121 – 180 AD)

When they got back to the Tahoe, they hooked the handcuffs on Novak's wrists to a D-ring that was bolted to the floor in the back seat. They did this with a short piece of chain Sonny carried for that purpose.

"What about my truck?" Novak scowled.

"Not our problem," Sonny said. "Talk to someone when you get to the Hennepin County jail."

They were headed south on Hwy. 169, going around the west side of Mille Lacs Lake through Garrison, when Sonny said, "Give a call to Saul's office, would ya? He'll have gone home by the time we get back there, but I'm sure he'd love to hear the good news."

Dillon picked up his phone to punch in Saul's number, then Sonny held up his hand, saying, "Wait just a sec, Dillon."

Dillon cancelled the call and looked at Sonny. "Yeah?"

"Since rounding up Novak came off pretty easy, what would you think of charging Saul just a fifteen percent fee, instead of our usual nineteen percent when it's a risky character?"

"I've got no problem with that," Dillon said. "Still a big payday on a bond that size."

"That's what I was thinking, too. I'm sure Saul would be very grateful."

Returning to his phone, Dillon reached Saul, who was indeed very grateful. Grateful they had captured Novak so quickly, and grateful that they were reducing their fee a bit. "I'll be headed for home before you get back here," Saul said, "but I'll leave a check with Deb. She's working until Johnny comes in at eight o'clock for the night shift. Give her your paperwork and she'll give you the check. Thanks again, you made my whole week."

"Hope to see you soon," Dillon said, then hung up the phone.

"I couldn't hear it all, but it sounded like Saul was grateful like we figured," Sonny said.

"He sure was. And he's leaving a check for us with Deb. We can go pick it up this evening if you want."

"Sure do. We'll drop Novak at Hennepin County, swing by Saul's office to get the check, then back to my place and I'll write you a check."

"That'll be great," Dillon said. "It'll sure help my checking account balance."

After some fun flirting with Deb at Saul's office, Sonny and Dillon headed toward Sonny's bank on Central Avenue to put the check in the night deposit box. As they crossed the Third Avenue Bridge, Sonny said, "Take a look at the black Camaro following us, this is the third time I've noticed it in the last two weeks."

Dillon turned to look out the rear window, then turned back and leaned forward to look at the side mirror. "The one two cars back. Behind the blue-and-white cab... that's right behind us?" he asked.

34

"Yeah, like I said, this is the second or third time I've noticed a vehicle like that behind me."

"Swing right at East Hennepin, then take a left on Eighth Street to get back to Central Avenue. See if he follows us all the way around," Dillon said, staring at the side mirror.

Sonny took East Hennepin to Eighth Street, then left to Central and right towards his bank. The black Camaro lagged a ways behind, but follow the same route.

"Yup, looks like he's following you all right," Dillon said. "He's pretty good, staying way behind like that. The average person wouldn't even notice him."

The Northeast Branch of US Bank is on the west side of Central just before 24th Avenue. As Sonny swung in the drive-thru, the black Camaro cruised past.

Leaving the bank, Sonny headed north on Central Avenue again and saw the black Camaro parked along the curb. As they passed Lowry Avenue, the Camaro pulled out and resumed following them.

"Next red light, let's get out and have a talk with this fellow," Dillon said. "See if you recognize him, or if we can find out anything about him."

Ahead, at 27th Avenue, the signal lights turned yellow, so Sonny stopped and put the Tahoe in park. They watched the Camaro slowing down, still nearly a block behind them. As he got closer, Sonny said, "Let's go." They both unbuckled their seatbelt, jumped from the vehicle and ran back toward the Camaro. The driver of the Camaro looked like he was going to stop, but then suddenly gunned it and nearly hit Dillon, who dove to the side.

Sonny immediately drew his Glock, took aim, but then slowly lowered it again. With other traffic and pedestrians in the area, he didn't want to chance a shot at the Camaro. He holstered the Glock and looked toward Dillon, who was picking himself up off the pavement and glaring in the direction of the accelerating car.

"You okay, Dillon?"

"Yeah. I'm okay. But that guy's not going to be if I ever get my hands on him."

At Sonny's home, they sat at his kitchen table opening a beer and talking about the character in the black Camaro. "No idea who it could be?" Dillon asked. "No threats? Nothing?"

"No, I don't recognize the Camaro at all, and have no idea who the guy is. I'm guessing that it's something to do with a bail skip I hauled in."

"Well... we're just gonna have to keep our eyes peeled until we can figure the guy out," Dillon said, shrugging his shoulders then downing more of his beer. "I've been telling you for the last couple years that you need a security system in your home here. Maybe it's time you get one."

"Yeah, you're probably right. I don't need to come home some night and find that guy sitting in my recliner with a shotgun pointed at me."

The next morning, Sonny was on the phone with his friend, J.R., who sold and installed security systems, and who had also been trying to convince Sonny for a couple years that he needed one in his home. "Tomorrow afternoon? That'd be great J.R. See you at two o'clock."

After J.R. had installed the system and walked him through how everything worked, Sonny was more than a little impressed. He was amazed he could control everything from his cell phone and watch his home on his phone through closed-circuit cameras. He could even talk to or yell at potential intruders. He was surprised how good it felt knowing he could watch his home from anywhere.

Sonny called Sonja and got her voice mail. "I hope you're move is going good. Just wanted to let you know that I finally took your advice, and that of several of my friends, and had a security system installed in my home. I'll plan on seeing you in three days. Call and let me know if you're going to be delayed. Love you, Babe."

Sonny shut off his phone and looked down at the photo of Sonja on the screen. It was one of his favorites. It not only showed how gorgeous she was, but showed the twinkle in her eyes and the sweetness in her smile.

The "move" Sonny had referred to, was Sonja moving a wealthy family from Apple Valley to St. George, Utah. Sonja's company – Precision Movers – specialized in moving delicate, expensive items. She regularly helped companies, families, or individuals move medical equipment, computers, communication equipment, photo lab equipment, expensive art and antiques, large collections of valuable items, even large wine collections.

The family she was moving to St. George, Utah had a very expensive grand piano, a large collection of artwork, and a number of antiques that would all require special handling. The wife was familiar with Sonja's company, and would hire them only if Sonja herself supervised the entire move, start to finish. Sonja agreed.

Her company owned two tractor-trailer rigs and two large van trucks, equipped with special air ride systems and climate control systems. She had a shop and staff that could custom-build crates to handle virtually anything fragile.

Sonny had always been amazed by Sonja and how she got to the position of "Owner and President of Precision Movers." She spent her first year of college at St. Catherine University in St. Paul. That spring, looking for a summer job that paid well, a friend who owned a dump truck and worked for one of the largest highway construction companies in Minnesota, told her the company was hiring women drivers. "Think you can handle it?" he asked.

"Don't know. Never tried it."

"If you'd like to try, I can teach you on weekends with my truck. The job gets a lot of hours and the pay is really good. Then there's a couple months lay-off every winter."

So, she spent the next few weekends learning how to handle a tandem axle dump truck, and was hired by the company and told to come to work the day after school was out for the summer. She was one of their lead drivers by the end of that summer, and decided not to go back to school. During the next year she moved up to tri-axle dump trucks, then tractor-trailer rigs with side dump, belly dump, and end dump trailers. Occasionally, she even drove a low-boy, hauling pieces of heavy equipment.

She heard about the need for "specialty" movers and thought, "Why not me?" The end result was her establishing "Precision Movers" during the next six months.

Chapter Seven

"The happiness of your life depends upon the quality of your thoughts."
Marcus Aurelius (121 – 180 AD)

The following morning, Sonny was eating breakfast and his phone rang. He glanced at the caller ID and saw 'Assured Bail Bonds,' another client that he did a fair amount of skip work for. He picked up his phone and tapped the button to answer the call. "Good morning," he said brightly.

"Good morning, Sonny. This is Max Schulman."

"Hey Max, great to hear from you."

"Got a minute to talk, Sonny?"

"For you Max, I got all the time in the world," Sonny said, with as much flattery as he could muster.

"It's nice to be held in such high esteem," Max said, then laughed.

"Only for you, Max. Only for you."

"Okay... enough of the bull," Max said. "I got a skip that needs rounding up, and I let this one get down to the wire. We got less than three weeks to bring him in, or I pony up thirty thousand dollars to the court. Can you help me out on short notice like this?"

"Your timing is perfect. My calendar is open for the next couple weeks," Sonny said, cringing when he thought about putting his trip with Sonja on hold again. But he owed Max one, and knew Sonja would forgive him.

Later that morning, looking through the file Max gave him, Donald Eckhard, the skip, was owner of Eckhard Accounting with his son James. Donald was up on charges of "Estafa through Fraud" – basically he had swindled a client out of a property.

From everything he could see in the file, including a photo of Eckhard showing him to be a rather slight, good looking man, Sonny didn't see him posing any physical danger. The first thing that caught his eye was reference to a condominium that he owned together with his brother and sister in Sedona, Arizona.

Sonny had a good friend who owned a small art shop in Sedona, and had lived there for maybe a dozen years. He called him and asked, "Jim, do you know where Jason Road is in Sedona?"

"Sure do. What'aya need?"

"Well, there's a guy I'm looking for that's one of the owners of the condominium at 270 Jason Road, unit A-1. I'd like to know if there's anyone staying there right now. Can you check it out for me?"

"Sure can," Jim said.

"I'll scan and send you a photo of the guy that I'm looking for."

"That'll be great," Jim said. "If it looks like anyone's there, I'll knock on the door and say I must have the wrong address, because he doesn't look like the fellow who bought this painting I'm delivering."

"That works! I knew I could count on you, Jim. Give me a call as soon as you have anything."

"I will. It's the least I can do... for you tracking down the guy that swindled our daughter out of two thousand dollars last year."

That evening, Sonny's phone rang and he saw Jim's name on the caller ID. He was excited to hear back from him so quickly and grabbed his phone. "Hey Jim... any luck?"

"Yeah, I went by early this afternoon and there was no one there. After I thought about it a while, I figured he may be a golfer and might be home later in the day. I went by there at five o'clock and Bingo! The guy, whose picture you sent me, answered the door.

"I came all prepared though," Jim continued. "You'd've been proud of me. I'd looked up the name of a client who had bought some artwork from me and lived on Jason Road. I said I must have the wrong address and asked him if he knew Mr. Ron Henderson who lived in the same group of condominiums?

"When he said no, I said, Well, I'll have to go back to the shop and get the correct address from the paperwork on his order. Sorry to bother you."

"'No bother at all,' the guy said. So, once I was away from his home, I called you."

"Great work, Jim. I'm going to catch a plane first thing in the morning to Flagstaff. Any chance I can hire you to pick me up at the airport?

"Hire nothing," Jim insisted. "Just leave me a message with the time you're going to be arriving and I'll be there to pick you up."

"Thanks again, Jim. See you tomorrow."

41

At nine o'clock the next morning, Sonny left a message on Jim's phone that he would be landing about three-fifteen that afternoon, and would call when they landed to find out where he should meet him.

Jim found Sonny, and now they were headed to the Coconino County Sheriff's Office in Flagstaff. "I need to let them know what I'm doing in their county, and that I hope to be escorting Eckhard back to Minneapolis.

After visiting the sheriff's office, they headed south on Hwy 89A and would be in Sedona in about forty-five minutes. "Do you wanna head right for the condominium?" Jim asked.

"Yeah, let's check if anyone's home today."

"I swung by there before coming to the airport," Jim said. "He was home and, with the light rain this afternoon, I don't think he'll be golfing."

Sonny smiled at Jim, then said, "If you ever need a job, come back to Minneapolis and work with me."

Chapter Eight

"No man is happy who does not think himself so."
Marcus Aurelius (121 – 180 AD)

As they neared Eckhard's condo, Sonny said, "Pull right into his drive and up to his garage door to block any chance of him trying to get away in his car."

"Got'cha," Paul said quietly.

As they got to the driveway, Paul turned in and eased his car up near the garage door. Sonny quickly got out, walked to the front door and pressed the doorbell button.

Soon the door was opening and Sonny immediately recognized Eckhard, who started to say, "Can I...." His voice trailed off, as recognition began to show in his eyes. "You're that bounty hunter," he said, his shoulders slumping.

"I am," Sonny said. "And I'm here to take you back to Minneapolis."

"Guess it was mighty foolish, thinking you wouldn't find me here," Eckhard said with resignation. "I won't give you any trouble," he said. "Can I have a second to grab my wallet 'n stuff from the bedroom?"

"I guess so," Sonny said, "since you say you'll give me no trouble." He watched Eckhard walk away and down the hallway to the bedroom... he supposed. In a few seconds, he heard the high pitched whine of what sounded like a dirt bike starting in the garage. He ran around the corner and down the hallway where Eckhard had gone, and saw the door leading to the garage partly open.

Sonny quickly pushed it all the way open, just in time to see the trail of exhaust smoke leading out the side door of the garage. He ran to the door to see where the bike and the lying Eckhard had gone. He ripped down the slope and across the backyard, toward who knows what, leaving a trail of torn up turf.

Just then, Paul came around the corner of the garage and saw Sonny standing there, hands on his hips and slowly shaking his head.

"What happened?" Paul asked.

"Bamboozled me, then he scooted through the backyard on a dirt bike," Sonny said. "Any idea where it leads?" he asked, looking back at Paul.

Quickly turning and heading back to his car, Paul shouted, "Yup! Let's go!"

Sonny had barely slammed his door shut, when Paul was backing out of the driveway and screeching up the street the same direction that Eckhard had gone. "This area is kind of like a small box canyon, and the only way out is at the far end near the clubhouse of the golf course."

Snapping his seatbelt, Sonny said, "Sure glad you're with me. I wouldn't know where he was headed."

After a bit, Sonny said, "My own fault."

"What is?" Paul asked, glancing toward Sonny.

"That he got away like he did. I should have cuffed him first, then taken him to get his wallet and other stuff. I let my guard down when he gave me the 'whipped puppy' routine."

The tires on Paul's car squealed loudly as he swung into the parking of the golf course. Just then, the dirt bike came flying around the far side of the clubhouse and ripped across the large putting green, with Eckhard crouched low on the bike. Paul quickly swung to cut him off before he could leave the parking lot. As he closed in on Eckhard, he pushed open the driver's door and slammed it into the bike, sending Eckhard and the dirt bike sliding across the parking lot.

He jammed on his brakes and Sonny jumped from the car. "Don't you move," Sonny shouted angrily. "Don't even blink... or I'll put'cher lights out for ya." He ran to Eckhard and roughly cuffed his hands behind his back.

Sonny stood and looked at Paul. "That was some good driving. I'll pay for the repair of your door."

"Don't worry about it. My insurance will take care of it. Besides, that was kind of fun!"

"Yeah," Sonny said, laughing. "Did you think you were in some kind of Steve McQueen movie or something?"

"Yeah, and I was his co-star," Paul said, smiling.

"Not many skips come this easy. But I've been on a lucky streak lately," Sonny said. "Can I trouble you one more time, and get a ride for me and this character back to the Flagstaff airport?"

"You sure can. And it's no trouble at all," Paul said.

"Well, after this escapade, I'd say you balanced the books. You don't owe me anything more."

"I'm not so sure," Paul said. "This was so much fun that I think I still owe you."

"No... we're all square. Next time you and Kathy come to Minnesota, dinner is on me. No arguing."

On the way to the airport, Sonny reserved two tickets to Minneapolis, and explained that he was transporting a handcuffed prisoner. "He will be no danger to anyone, though," Sonny explained. As usual, their seats would be in the last row, with the prisoner seated in the window seat.

Chapter Nine

"If it is not right do not do it; if it is not true do not say it."
Marcus Aurelius (121 – 180 AD)

After a brief stop at the Coconino County Sheriff's office, Paul took Sonny and Eckhard to the airport. They had nearly three hours to kill before their flight, so they sat at a café table having a bite to eat. Sonny took advantage of the time to check on flights to and from St. Thomas Island, then called Sonja.

"Hi Babe," he said when he heard her voice. "I'm doing great" he said, answering her question. "I'll be flying back tonight with my guy in cuffs." He paused, listening, then said, "Yup, I wanted to check and be sure you're still okay with taking next week off at work. If you can, we'll fly out Saturday morning to St. Thomas and fly back the following Sunday afternoon."

Again he paused, listening, then said, "That's great! I just wanted to check with you before I booked everything. I'll call you tomorrow with the flight times and the other details." They talked for another ten minutes about small things, ordinary things, then he said, "Okay Babe. Love you too. See you tomorrow. We'll figure out some place to go out for dinner tomorrow night."

When he shut off his phone and put it in his pocket, Eckhard said "Must've been your sweetheart, huh? Or is she your fiancé?"

Sonny glared at him, then growled, "Did someone tell you that you could talk?"

Eckhard shrank back in his seat with a look that said, *Sorry that I'm even breathing and wasting oxygen.*

Actually, Sonny was less concerned with whether it was Eckhard's business or not – which it wasn't – then he was with his continual effort to keep *anyone* from knowing who Sonja was or that he cared deeply for her. It had taken a bit for Sonja to understand and not be offended by this. In his line of work there was a very real possibility of someone threatening Sonja to get at him.

The flight back to Minneapolis was quiet and uneventful. At the Minneapolis airport, Sonny walked Eckhard across the sky-way to the parking ramp and his car. He put Eckhard in the back seat and chained the handcuffs to the D-ring bolted to the floor.

He drove up West 7th Street to downtown St. Paul and the Ramsey County jail. After completing the paperwork on Eckhard and driving to his home, it was three o'clock in the morning when he finally climbed into bed.

Chapter Ten

"Confine yourself to the present."
Marcus Aurelius (121 – 180 AD)

That Saturday morning, Sonny drove to Sonja's home in Eagan to pick her up, then on to the airport where they had a nice breakfast while waiting for their departure time. They would fly to Fort Lauderdale, Florida, then on to St. Thomas. On the island they would be staying at the Bolongo Bay Hotel. Sonny had told Sonja he had a friend who worked at the hotel, so he could get a bit of a deal. What he hadn't said was that his friend, Steve, was the hotel manager. But... that was Sonny. He generally understated most things, not ever wanting to feel that he was being boastful.

Sonja set her coffee cup down, saying, "I know I'm bad with how much I'm on the phone and the computer, but sometimes I think you're just as bad."

Sonny started to object, and Sonja put up her hands to interrupt him. "I know... I know. We've debated this more than a few times. That's not my point right now. Were both a little bad, but the nature of our work kind of makes it be that way. This is going to be our beautiful, tropical vacation as the snow is beginning to fly in Minnesota. So... I'm suggesting we make it a no-tech week. No phones, no computers, no technology for a week."

"I really like the idea, if we could make just one slight modification."

"And that is?" Sonja said, her head tilted and a questioning look on her face.

49

"That we set aside one hour on Wednesday morning, say eleven 'til noon, to check messages and emails and make any calls that are needed."

"Deal," Sonja said, extending her hand to shake Sonny's.

"Deal," Sonny said, gently taking her hand and kissing it softly.

Their flights to Fort Lauderdale and on to St. Thomas went smoothly. They checked into the Bolongo Bay Hotel and were extremely impressed with the suite they would be staying in.

"Wow" Sonja said spinning and looking all around. "Look at this place!" Then, opening the patio door to the veranda, she said, with the same enthusiasm, "And look at this gorgeous, gorgeous view!"

Sonny, slowly following her, smiled and gave her a hug. "Yes, the view is gorgeous," he said staring into her eyes. Then looking out to the ocean, he added, "The Atlantic's not bad either."

"Oh you," she said, slapping him lightly on the chest.

"How about we put on our swimsuits, go sit by a beach cabana and have a drink or two?" Sonny asked.

Sonja smiled and gave him a kiss on the cheek, saying, "Let's do it!"

The next four days were absolutely wonderful. Mixed in with lots of time relaxing in the sun, they did some snorkeling, some sailing, zip-lining, parasailing, and even a little fishing on a charter boat.

On Wednesday morning at eleven o'clock, as agreed, Sonny fired up his laptop and turned on his telephone. Sonja was doing the same.

Sonny had fifty-nine email messages and six phone messages. He deleted all but three of the emails and two of the phone messages. The first of the two phone messages was from Dave Hammer at Twin City Bail Bonds. He dialed Dave's direct line, heard him answer, then said, "Hey Dave, this is Sonny returning your call."

"Sonny, it's great to hear from you. What's your schedule like next week?"

"Next week is pretty open for me. I'm out of town until Monday, but good after that. What's up?"

"I've got one that I've let get down to the last few weeks and I figured I better get you on it before I run out of time. Any chance you can stop by my office Tuesday morning to look at the file?"

"How about eleven o'clock Tuesday morning?" Sonny asked. "I'm relaxing on St. Thomas Island this week with a dear friend, and won't be back in full swing until then. Does that work for your schedule?"

"S-o-o-o... you're lounging in the sun, getting a nice tan, while we're getting six inches of snow," Dave said, then laughed. "Eleven o'clock is great for me on Tuesday morning. Enjoy the sun."

"I'll see you Tuesday at eleven."

"I look forward to seeing you then," Dave said and clicked off the call.

Sonny jotted some notes in his calendar. He was still a bit of a dinosaur in that area, liking an old-fashioned pocket calendar to write down his schedule and his case notes.

His second phone message was from Dominick De Luca of De Luca Bail Bonds in St. Louis. *Who is Dominick De Luca and how does he know me?* he wondered. Finally, he shrugged his shoulders and dialed the number.

"Dominick De Luca," he heard a voice say.

"Hi, this is Harrison Lee Sawyer Jr., better known to most as Sonny. I'm returning your call."

"Oh yes, Sonny. Thanks for calling. I've got a skip that I'm on the hook for a million if I don't round him up in the next two months. I've had my usual guy on it for more than a month and a half now and he's coming up blank. So, I checked with people I know in the business and your name kept coming up as the best. Any chance I can send you a copy of the file and see if you can help me find this jumper?"

"Sure thing. Send it and I'll let you know if I think I can help you. I won't be in my office until Tuesday afternoon, so you don't have to overnight it or anything."

"Okay. I'll send a copy of the complete file by regular mail so it will be at your office when you get there on Tuesday. The guy is a handful from East St. Louis and is up on voluntary manslaughter charges. He served two years on a previous aggravated assault charge and is facing a possible five to fifteen on this one, so it's no piece of cake. I'm willing to pay nineteen percent if you bring him in."

"Okay, I'll be back to you sometime Tuesday afternoon," Sonny said.

52

"Until that time," De Luca said, and hung up his phone.

Sonny sat back in his chair, staring out at the Atlantic, *Aggravated assault and now voluntary manslaughter? De Luca wasn't exaggerating a bit in saying this would be no piece of cake,* he thought. But he figured he and Dillon could handle it. And... it would be their biggest payday ever.

He searched the contact file in his phone and punched up Dillon's number. When he heard Dillon answer, he said, "Hey there, it's Sonny calling from beautiful, tropical St. Thomas Island."

"Sure, I suppose it's sunny and eighty down there, and you're getting a nice tan" Dillon grumbled, "while were getting six inches of snow."

"Ain't it wonderful!"

"Yeah... What's up?"

"Got a call out of the blue from a guy named Dave De Luca in St. Louis. He's the owner of De Luca Bail Bonds. Got my name from somewhere and wants to hire us for a skip that he has a million dollar bond out on. The guy has a few serious offenses, so it's probably going to be our toughest one ever. He's sending me the file and I thought you could come over and join me for dinner Tuesday and we'll have a look at it. See if it looks like something we can handle... something we want to handle.

"Oh... and one other thing," Sonny added. "he's willing to pay nineteen percent."

"Sounds real interesting," Dillon said, "I'll be at your place Tuesday at six."

"Okay. Caitlin had to rearrange her cleaning schedule for me, and will be there Tuesday. She's a great cook, so I think I'll see if I can bribe her to work a little later that evening... fix us a nice dinner."

"Sounds great," Dillon said. "Besides, Caitlin's real easy on the eyes."

Chapter Eleven

"Don't think of the not, rather think of the not yet."
Marcus Aurelius (121 – 180 AD)

The rest of their time on St. Thomas was wonderful, and the two lounged lazily in bed Sunday morning talking of the days they'd shared. Both were reluctant to climb out of bed and get ready to head for the airport.

Sonny's friend, Steve, had arranged transportation for them to the airport and was at the checkout desk to thank them. "I hope you truly enjoyed St. Thomas," Steve said, shaking hands with each of them.

"It was fantastic!" Sonja said. "We'll definitely be back again one day."

"Thanks, old friend," Sonny said. "Thanks for everything. And let us know the next time you're going to be in Minnesota visiting family. It would be fun to get together."

"It'll probably be next June sometime," Steve said. "I'll let you know as soon as we set the dates."

On the flight back to Ft. Lauderdale they looked through the dozens, probably hundreds, of digital photos they'd taken. "I'm going to have a bunch of these put into a photo album by Shutter Fly or somebody," Sonja said. "It'll be fun to have it to look back through once in a while."

"Yeah, that sounds like lots of fun," Sonny said, tipping his seat back to catch a short nap. Sonja pushed her's back as well, leaned toward Sonny and rested her head on his shoulder.

Late Monday morning, Sonny sat at his desk opening mail. He'd placed the large envelope from De Luca Bail Bonds on the bottom of the stack, knowing that one would take some time to digest and decide if he wanted to take on the job of tracking down and bringing in this guy from East St. Louis. He wasn't worried about taking on the skip, but how many "friends" does he have that might get involved?

Finally, he'd opened and sorted all of his mail and only the brown envelope with the name De Luca Bail Bonds printed in large, bold letters lay on his desk. He grabbed it, slit the end open with his letter opener, removed the thick file of papers and began reading about Juan Esteban Garcia, better known as "Little Johnny."

Little Johnny had a fairly long list of offenses. The most recent, and most serious, was his conviction for aggravated assault for which he served a little over two years at USP Marion in southern Illinois. His last known residence was near North 23rd Street and Benton Avenue in the Hyde Park area. He was five foot eleven, two hundred twenty pounds, and the photo in the file showed him to be very strong built, with ink covering most of his arms and neck.

Sonny leaned back, staring at the photo. *Looks like we might be getting acquainted, Little Johnny*, he thought, then called Dillon. "Caitlin wasn't able to stay late; can you pick up some dinner on your way over?"

That evening, about ten minutes to six, Dillon rang Sonny's doorbell with his elbow, his hands full of their dinner from LeeAnn Chin's. He was carrying containers of Pork fried rice, Peking chicken, Beef and broccoli, and Lo mein. As they finished eating, Sonny handed him the file, pointing out the items he'd highlighted.

"It's definitely going to be one of our biggest challenges... since DeLuca's guy has been on it for nearly two months and come up empty," Sonny said, wiping his fingers on a napkin and throwing it on the table. "It doesn't say anywhere in the file that he's a gang member. If he is, who knows what we may run up against? But... this would be our biggest payday ever, so I say we go after it."

"I'm in," Dillon said without hesitation.

Late Tuesday morning, Sonny was headed toward the offices of Twin City Bail Bonds and his eleven o'clock appointment with Dale Hammer. Dale escorted him back to his office and pointed to a chair. Then he reached across his desk for a file marked 'Stephen Briggs' and handed it to Sonny. He took a chair beside him, saying, "This one shouldn't be too big a deal for you, but I let it get down to the wire hoping that he might get picked up by local police for speeding... anything."

As Sonny glanced through the file, he said, "Second DWI for him?"

"Yeah," Dale said, "and he's only looking at a one year license revocation, maybe serving thirty to sixty days, so I don't know why he's making a bigger problem for himself by not showing."

"So," Sonny said, "looks like we've got twenty days until your time's up with the court. I think I can round him up for you. I'd have to charge you nineteen percent plus any unusual expenses."

"That's about what I expected," Dale said. "I've got a copy of your list of Unusuals in my file. I'll be glad when we can finally scratch this guy off our board."

Sonny left Dale's office and headed up University Avenue to Shaw's to grab a burger for lunch. Shaw's was the old Sun Saloon where he'd first met Saul Berkowitz, and they still served his favorite burgers.

After lunch, he ran home to pick up a few things, and then spent the rest of that afternoon and early evening watching Stephen Briggs' home on Lyndale Avenue South in Richfield. He parked where he could watch the front door and see through the backyard to the garage. For nearly four hours he watched and saw no one come or go. Finally, he got out of his car, pulled on a blue windbreaker – mostly to hide his side arm – grabbed a clipboard and walked to the front door. He rang the doorbell and waited. After a bit, he rang the doorbell again and looked at the mailbox as he waited.

When no one answered, he glanced around to be sure no neighbors were walking by, then grabbed the mail and rifled through it. Most of it was less than a week old, and all of it was addressed to Stephen Briggs. *There must be no wife or kids?* Sonny thought. He stuffed the phone bill in his pocket, replaced the rest of the mail and returned to his car.

He sat looking through Briggs' file, searching for his place of employment. Sonny was sure he'd seen it before, but couldn't remember for sure. Finally he found it. Jimmy's Place, where he'd tended bar for almost five years. Jimmy's was on University Avenue just off Snelling, so Sonny headed there to see what he could learn about Briggs.

Jimmy, the owner, was there and told Sonny that Briggs hadn't worked for a couple months now. "He said his mom was fighting cancer and he needed to go there to take care of her for a while. I was hoping that I would have heard from him by now."

"Do you know where his mom lives?" Sonny asked.

"New Richmond, Wisconsin, I think."

"New Richmond. That's a nice little town just a half hour east of Stillwater."

"Yeah, I'm pretty sure that's where he grew up, and I think she still lives there," Jimmy said with a shrug. "If I remember right, his dad passed away a couple years ago."

"Well, thanks for all your help Jimmy. If you hear from Steve, tell him that my name is Harrison and I'm trying to catch up with him and get his signature, so I can give him a couple thousand dollars tax refund. It was an error on one of his returns." Sonny jotted his name and cell phone number on a napkin and handed it to Jimmy.

"I'm sure he'll be happy to hear that," Jimmy said.

Sonny jumped in his car and headed for home to pack some stuff in case he had to spend a couple days in New Richmond. After packing, he headed east on Interstate 94 to Hudson, Wisconsin to check in with the St. Croix County Sheriff, then north to New Richmond where he checked in to the AmericInn motel.

The next morning, Sonny enjoyed a leisurely breakfast at a café not far from the motel. He planned on going to the City Hall to find out what he could about the Briggs family. At the New Richmond City Hall he found the city clerk's office, and found her very helpful. She said she had only been a casual acquaintance of Mrs. Briggs, but was sure she still lived in their family's home off 157th Avenue, east of Highway 65. "Here it is," she said, and read him the address from her computer screen.

He thanked her and, as he walked back to his car, studied the map she had sketched for him. He drove south of town and easily found the Briggs' home, pulled in the driveway and walked to the front door.

An older woman, who was wearing a baseball cap on her bald head – bald from the cancer treatments she was enduring, Sonny figured – answered the door and, smiling said, "Can I help you?"

"Hi. My name is Harrison Sawyer. Are you Mrs. Briggs?"

"I'm Harriet Briggs. How can I help you Mr. Sawyer?"

"Well, I was hoping to find your son Steve here. I was told he was helping you through your cancer treatments."

"Yes, he's been a great help and comfort to me," she said, stepping aside and waving her hand to invite Sonny into her home. "He ran to town to pick up a few things at the grocery store, but should be back in a few minutes if you'd like to wait."

"Thank you so much Mrs. Briggs... Harriet," Sonny said, returning her smile.

"I was working on some stuff in the kitchen, if you don't mind waiting with me in there."

"I don't mind at all," Sonny said, and followed her to the kitchen.

Harriet was a very pleasant woman to be around, and very easy to carry on a conversation with. Soon, a car was pulling in the driveway, and she said, "Oh, there comes Steven now."

Sonny watched Briggs closely as he got out of his car. He glanced at Sonny's car, but didn't seem to be at all alarmed as he grabbed the bags of groceries from the back seat. He came up the steps to the side door and into the kitchen. Setting the bags on the counter, he said, "Hello, I'm Steve... and you are?"

"I'm Harrison Sawyer and I've got some tax papers for you to sign. No need for concern though, I've got a fairly nice refund for you."

"Well! That's a bit of good news, isn't it mom," Steve said, smiling at his mom.

Walking toward the door, Sonny said, "Why don't you come out to my car with me, sign a couple of forms, and I'll get the IRS to send a check out to you tomorrow."

As they reached his car, Sonny turned to face Briggs with a serious look. "I'm not with the IRS. I'm here to bring you back to Twin City Bail Bonds and your court appearance in Hennepin County."

He watched Briggs' shoulders slump and the color drain from his face. Then he held his hands up toward Briggs as though trying to ease his fears, saying, "But I'd like to help you out... or rather... help your mom out, so she doesn't have to know about your troubles. She's got enough already."

"What are you saying?" Briggs asked.

"I'm saying I've got to bring you in, but I'll give you a week to help your mom and explain to her why you have to go back home for a bit. Then you show up at Twin City Bail Bonds next Friday morning at 8 o'clock. Can I trust you enough that you'll show up this time?"

Briggs was noticeably relieved, and said, "Mom's cancer was the only reason I didn't show the first time. It's been a rough couple months for her, and I knew she would need my help. Give me next week, like you said, to work things out and I'll be there Friday morning."

Sonny extended his hand, shook Steve's and said, "Okay. I'll let Dale Hammer know that you'll be in his office in a week... first thing that Friday morning. If I have to come after you again, you won't like it one bit."

"I'm sure I wouldn't," Steve said, smiling at Sonny. "I'll be there."

On the way back to his motel room, Sonny called Dale Hammer and explained the circumstance with Stephen Briggs. "I believed him when he said the only reason he missed his court appearance was because he was here helping his mom through her cancer treatment. And, I guess, I believe that he will show up Friday morning next week."

"Let's hope for the best... for everyone," Dale said. "See you next Friday."

Chapter Twelve

"Waste no time debating what a good man should be. Just be one."
Marcus Aurelius (121 – 180 AD)

That afternoon, Sonny checked out of the motel and was headed back home. He was thinking about Harriet and so glad he'd had the chance to meet her and visit with her. It cast a whole new light on Steve and the kind of man he was. It wasn't often that this job gave him a nice kind of personal satisfaction, but giving Steve the benefit of the doubt, and time to work things out, gave Sonny a great sense of having helped them in a real good way.

Not the same kind of satisfaction I'll get when we've brought Little Johnny into the St. Louis County jail, Sonny thought, turning his attention to his next skip trace and one of his most difficult, being a stranger to St. Louis.

Sonny wasn't sure why he was feeling so uptight about this skip. But that wasn't all bad. "Hopefully it'll keep me sharp and on my toes," he said softly to himself.

During the hour and a half ride home, Sonny kept thinking through the details of Little Johnny's file. Every time he tried to formulate a plan, he'd run into another dead-end. *Sometimes you just have to put your feet on the ground and see where the leads take you,* he thought.

Trying to relax and clear his mind, he reached and turned up the volume of the CD that was playing. He was a lover of classic country music and a CD of Hank Williams Sr. was playing his favorite Hank song, "Someday You'll Call My Name." He cranked it up loud.

Back at home, he sat down at his desk and phoned Dillon. "I spoke with DeLuca yesterday and told him we'd take the job. Can you be ready to leave my house by eight o'clock tomorrow morning?"

"I'll be there, ready to roll."

In the morning, they pulled out of Sonny's driveway a few minutes past eight. Dillon had picked up a large coffee for each of them, and a couple rolls and doughnuts to snack on as they headed south on Hwy. 61 toward St. Louis. Sonny planned to call DeLuca later that morning and let him know they would be arriving at his office about four o'clock in the afternoon.

Chapter Thirteen

"I do not regard a man as poor, if the little he has is enough for him."
Marcus Aurelius (121 – 180 AD)

"Our man, Jimmy Taylor, has run into more dead ends than I thought you could find in St. Louis," De Luca said, to start the afternoon meeting with Sonny and Dillon. "And he ends up with more questions than answers." He sighed, then swung from his desk chair and walked around his desk to sit with Sonny and Dillon. They sat at the glass-topped table that situated itself off the corner of his desk.

The glass top was strewn with photos and papers from Little Johnny's file. "Any idea where you'll start?" De Luca asked, pulling up a chair across from Sonny and Dillon, and plopping down in it.

"I haven't seen any notes from interviewing his mother, Camila Isabella Garcia," Sonny said. "Did Tyler ever mention anything?"

"Only that he didn't think a mother would give him anything on her son," De Luca answered. "

"Is your guy a rookie? One thing I've seen with most criminals is their love for, and loyalty to, their mother," Sonny said. "I think we'll start there tomorrow. See if she's still at the same address. If not, see if we can locate her."

"You'll keep me up to date?" De Luca asked.

"Yes sir, we will. Every Friday for sure, more often if we find things we think you should know. I'm certain there will be things we'll need your knowledge and help with, too."

The next morning they drove to the address of Camila Garcia, Juan's mother. Sonny knocked at the front door, while Dillon moved around to the back side, to see if anybody tried to leave through the rear door located at the back, right corner of the house.

A Hispanic woman, that Sonny guessed to be in her late thirties, opened the door. "Yes?" she said, questioningly.

"Hi. Is Mrs. Camila Garcia at home?" Sonny asked. "I have a small inheritance check for her."

"No. She has not lived here for about two years," the woman said.

"Oh, I'm sorry to trouble you, but do you know where she's moved to."

"Yes, she is my aunt, and she has moved to a smaller home just a couple blocks from here."

"Do you happen to have that address?"

"Yes, just a moment," the woman said, holding up her index finger and turning away. She quickly returned carrying an address book, and said, "She lives at 3927 Holder Ave. If you'd like, I could call and see if she is home right now?"

"Yes, that would be great. Thank you!"

Again, she held up an index finger, then turned and hurried away. He could hear her talking on her phone as she approached the door again. With her hand holding the edge of the door, she said, "Okay Auntie, I'm sure they'll stop by in a few minutes." Then, giving Sonny a bit of a smile, she said, "She's home. She was a little concerned, but I told her not to worry. That you seem to be very nice."

"Thank you," Sonny said, returning the smile. "That's very sweet of you, I appreciate it."

"And you better be very nice to her," the woman said sternly. "She is the best, kindest person I know."

"Thank you, so much. I will be extra nice to her," Sonny said, turning and moving down the steps. As he walked down the sidewalk, he glanced back and saw Dillon hurrying across the lawn toward him. As they crossed the street, Dillon softly asked, "Did you get anything on mom or where she's at?"

"Yup, got her address. And the lady called to see if she's home. She's there right now. Hop in."

They quickly drove the two and a half blocks to the address Sonny had jotted in his notebook. When they knocked on the door, a very pleasant, sixty-ish, Hispanic woman wearing a house dress and an apron, pleasantly answered the door.

"You must be the men my niece just called about."

"Yes, we are," Sonny said. "Would it be okay if we spoke with you for a bit about your son, Juan?"

She stepped aside, saying, "Please," and waved them in to her home. She closed the front door, walked across the room and sat in a rocker, saying, "How can I help you?"

Sonny paused a moment, a bit of a sad grin showing on his lips. "I'm not going to try and trick you... I don't have a check for you. I'm sure you know your son's been in some trouble. We've been hired by the De Luca Bail Bond company to find him and bring him back for his court hearing. Do you have any idea where he is at?"

"No, truthfully I haven't seen him in two months since he helped me fix my bathroom. And he hasn't called in three or four days." She was staring down at her hands as she spoke. Then, looking up at Sonny, she said, "I knew Johnny was in some kind of trouble again, the way he was dodging around all my questions when he helped me."

Sonny nodded, acknowledging Mrs. Garcia's intuition. "Somebody from Kansas City posted a very large bail bond for him. Any idea who this guy might be?"

"No, I don't know any of those Kansas City people. My husband used to have friends there, and Johnny has spent a lot of time there in recent years, too."

"Your husband? Mister Garcia?" Sonny asked.

"Well, yes and no. His name was Carl Brown. He was black... African-American. After we met and started dating, he got into big trouble with some people on the east side of Kansas City. So, when we got married, he changed his name to mine, Garcia, and we moved from Raytown to St. Louis. He hoped all this would keep them from finding him, and it worked. Who would guess a man would take the woman's name in marriage?" She slowly shook her head side to side, a soft smile showing on her lips.

"Well, anyway," she said, shaking off the sadness, "for years Carl would go back to Kansas City every once in a while to play poker and party with his buddies. Then Johnny, when he was an older teenager, started going there with him and got hooked up with some guys. I heard the name 'Latin Eagles' mentioned a couple times over the years. I figured it was some sort of gang, but by then Johnny was twenty years old and didn't want his mother telling him what he could do or not do."

"Is Mr. Garcia still around?" Sonny asked.

"Carl died from a heart attack three years ago, while Johnny was still in prison."

"I'm so sorry," Sonny said. "So, I guess you'd have no idea where Johnny stays when he's in Kansas City."

"No... none at all." She paused, staring out her front window for a few moments, then said, "He did mention once that there's a restaurant that serves good barbeque just down the block from his friend's apartment. But I'm sure that's not much help for you in a huge place like Kansas City."

"It's hard to say," Sonny told her. "But you never know. Thanks so much for inviting us into your home and speaking with us." He stood and reached out his hand to shake hers.

Dillon did the same, and as they turned to leave she said, "If I give you my phone number would you call me and let me know what's happening with Johnny?"

"Yes I would. I would be happy to do that."

They walked to her front door and as they opened it to leave, she gave them each a hug and a soft thank you. "You boys take care now. And, please, be easy on my son."

"What a sweet mom," Dillon said, as they headed down the sidewalk towards Sonny's vehicle.

"She sure is. I hope we don't have to call her and say things got rough with Johnny."

"Yeah, hopefully some of the sweetness in mom rubbed off on the son," Dillon said, opening the door and climbing in the Tahoe.

69

Sonny pressed himself against the back of the seat for a moment, staring out the windshield.

"What'cha contemplating?" Dillon asked.

"I'm thinking that since mom hasn't seen him for two months, Johnny's most likely in Kansas City. No sense finding a room here. Let's head for Kansas City."

"I saw a sign for Interstate 70 heading west," Dillon said. "Turn right up here and I think we'll find it. We can get a room along the way if we get tired."

Chapter Thirteen

"Does lack of admiration cause the emerald to lose beauty?"
Marcus Aurelius (121 – 180 AD)

They made it as far as Columbia, Missouri, that evening and decided it was as good a place as any to get a room and have a late bite to eat. The next morning they had breakfast at a Denny's restaurant, got some coffee for the road and headed for Kansas City.

Along the way, Dillon googled east side Kansas City restaurants and found more than three dozen. "There's six or seven that might serve good barbeque, so we might as well start with those," he said, jotting down the addresses.

They reached Kansas City and drove to the first address on Dillon's list. There they found a corner restaurant. "It's early for the lunch crowd, so maybe we can find the owner or someone who recognizes Johnny's picture," Dillon said, climbing out of the Tahoe and stretching.

In the restaurant, they showed the first employee who spoke with them the picture of Juan Garcia, asking, "Have you ever seen this man?"

"No, don't recognize him at all," the woman said.

"Is your boss here?" Sonny asked, smiling at her.

"Yes. Just-a-minute," she said, and hurried away toward the kitchen. In moments she was returning, followed by a thick built, older gentleman.

"How can I help you?" he asked politely.

Sonny smiled at him, then showed him the picture of Garcia. "We were wondering if you've ever seen this man."

The owner studied the picture for a few moments, looked at his waitress who was shaking her head, then said, "No, I don't remember ever seeing him before."

"Okay," Sonny said, reaching to shake his hand. "Thank you for taking the time to help us."

"You're very welcome," he said. "You come back 'n eat with us one day. We serve great barbeque!"

Getting back in the Tahoe, Dillon looked at his list and, as he drew a line through the first restaurant's name and address, said, "That's one down. Let's go straight ahead about five blocks. The next one should be on the right."

They repeated the same scenario at the second restaurant with the same outcome. Again Dillon drew a line through the name and address of the restaurant. "Straight ahead for three blocks, then left two blocks," he said.

This was repeated until the sixth restaurant on the list. When they showed the owner/chef – Dave of Dave's Diner – the photograph, he paused a few moments, then said, "Yeah, he's eaten here a few times and he's picked up 'to-go' orders, too. Why you lookin' for him?"

"Some trouble back in St. Louis. He missed a court date and we've been hired to get him back to court there."

"So, you're bail agents?" the man asked.

"Bail Agent... Fugitive Recovery Agent... Bounty Hunter... whatever label you'd like. I kind of prefer Skip Tracer myself," Sonny told him.

Reaching in his pocket, Sonny brought out a business card and handed it to Dave. "Next time you see him, call me right away. If we pick him up on your lead, there's a five hundred dollar cash reward. So, if he comes in, stall his meal or his to-go order for ten minutes, and we'll be here to pick him up and pay you the reward."

"Five hundred huh? Cash?" the owner asked, his eyes brightening.

"Cash on delivery," Sonny said.

They found a room in the Ashland Motel, which was less than ten minutes from the restaurant. Even though it was along Independence Avenue, one of the roughest areas in Kansas City – at least according to Google and news reports – the building looked fairly new and the rooms were fairly nice... and clean.

They decided to relax for a couple hours that afternoon, then stakeout the restaurant for the evening on the off chance that Garcia showed up. Tomorrow they would start going door to door in the area looking for Garcia. Anyone who knew him, anyone who recognized him from the photo, anything at all on Little Johnny.

At a little past four o'clock, Sonny climbed in the shower to freshen up and wake himself up. As soon as he was done, Dillon did the same. At five-thirty they drove over to Dave's Diner to try his cooking.

An attractive middle-aged waitress took their orders and brought them each a beer. Dave, the owner, came out of the kitchen smiling and shook their hands. "I just noticed you sitting here. Nice to see you again. Glad you came back for dinner!"

"We had to see if the food's as good as the aroma," Dillon said.

"You won't be disappointed." Dave patted Dillon on the shoulder, adding, "But I better get back in the kitchen so your ribs don't get overcooked."

Sonny and Dillon both enjoyed their dinners, and complemented Dave as they were leaving. Then Sonny said, quietly, "And like I said before, we'll be in the area so if you see anything of Garcia, call me right away."

Dave nodded and headed back to his kitchen.

The rest of that evening, until Dave closed his diner at ten-thirty, they parked down the block and across the street where they could easily see the people coming and going.

They saw no sign of Garcia all evening, and at quarter to eleven they stopped at Elva's Lounge for a nightcap. Waiting for the first drink, Dillon asked, "What time do you want to start knocking on doors tomorrow?"

"Oh, maybe around eleven. The late-nighters should be stirring by then."

By eleven-thirty the next morning, they had knocked on several doors with mixed reactions. One was very cooperative, almost pleasant, saying, "No, I don't think I know him. But if you leave a number, I'll call you if I see him." Another said, "No," and closed the door. Another said, "No! Now get the hell away from my door," and slammed it.

"I'm sure I don't have to tell you to be on the alert. One of these people is bound to pull a shotgun on us," Sonny said, as they walked up a broken sidewalk toward the next front door.

It took a little over an hour to cover the homes on one side of the block, then they crossed over and started back the other direction. About the fourth door they knocked on, as they were headed back, a Hispanic woman answered the door and politely told them, "No, I don't recognize him at all. Can I ask why you are looking for him?"

"Yes, you certainly can," Sonny said. "An aunt of Juan's passed away and left him several thousand dollars inheritance. We work for the Berkowitz Law Firm and are making one last effort to locate him. Then the inheritance will go to his mother."

"Okay," she said. "I'm just nosy I guess."

Sonny handed her a business card. "If you happen to see him, call me or let him know... or both," he said, nodding and turning to leave.

As they walked away from the door, Dillon said, "Hey, let me see that file."

Handing it to him, Sonny asked, "What's up?"

"One of the photos of Garcia has a guy partly visible in the background. When she opened the door, I think I saw that guy hurry from the kitchen." Then, tapping at the photo, he said, "That guy... that guy right there!"

"You sure?"

"Yup. I'm sure. This was the guy in her kitchen."

Sonny slapped him on the shoulder, saying, "You impress me more all the time, partner. That house will be our stakeout for the next couple days. Let's figure out the best spots front and back."

They located what they thought were the best places for surveillance. The first was on the street sitting in the Tahoe, watching the front door. The other was in back across the alley, with a couple bushes near a neighbor's garage for cover. They would trade off every half hour to keep each other alert.

They drove until they found a convenience store and picked up a few snacks to carry them through that afternoon and night until about two in the morning, when they'd go back to their room to sleep and start over in tomorrow.

Chapter Fifteen

"Do not be ashamed of needing help."
Marcus Aurelius (121 – 180 AD)

That first day, spent quietly watching the house, was very uneventful with not a soul coming or going. Dillon called it, "B-o-o-r-ring!"

"I know," Sonny told him. "But do you want boring or something real exciting, like gunfire?"

"Yeah, yeah, yeah... I'll take the boring stuff. But you'd think there'd be a few people coming or going or something, wouldn't-cha?"

"Maybe tonight," Sonny said, shrugging. "Go get in the truck. And stay alert."

"Okay," Dillon said with a smirk.

Sonny moved to the alley, sat down on the bucket behind the bushes, then leaned against the neighbor's garage and stared at the back door across the alley... the back door of the house where they hoped to find Garcia.

That night was not as boring, with quite a few people coming and going, but it wasn't any more productive. No sign of Garcia or the guy Dillon had seen that afternoon. About quarter past two in the morning, Dillon and Sonny were walking in the door of their motel room, both looking forward to a good night's sleep.

"I'm setting the clock for seven thirty. We can have a good breakfast and be out there by nine-thirty," Sonny said.

"Good by me," Dillon said, then flopped on his bed face down. As he turned his head on the pillow, he said, "Good night," and was soon breathing very heavily and very slowly. Sonny smiled, crawled into his bed, and soon was breathing in concert with Dillon.

After breakfast the next morning, Sonny drove down the alley and dropped Dillon off about two houses away from their target house. "See you in about a half-hour," Sonny said, then eased his way down the alley and around the block to where they had parked yesterday.

The street where they parked the Tahoe was lined with beautiful, large elm trees down both sides, so the Tahoe sat in the shade all day and stayed comfortable. Plus, with the shade of the elm trees and the heavy tinting on the windows, it was difficult to see that someone was sitting inside the vehicle.

After a half hour, Dillon was tapping on the window of the driver's door. The door opened quietly and Sonny slid out. Their routine had been for the one in the alley to walk down two houses, cut through a neighbor's yard and out to the street, then down to the Tahoe. The location of windows on the house they were watching made it almost impossible for anyone inside to see them switching.

"Gonna be a beautiful day," Dillon said. "Mostly sunny, with big fluffy clouds floating by. I really love spending it this way. Don't you?"

Sonny grinned, as he turned and walked away.

For the rest of that day, like yesterday, their radios were mostly silent since, other than regular check-ins, there wasn't anything going on for them to talk about.

That evening, as twilight set in over the neighborhood and darkness would soon be squeezing out the last of the sunlight, Sonny perked up as a car went past and swung to the curb, stopping in front of the house. Soon the front door opened and the fella from the photo stepped out. Then Garcia came out, following close behind.

Sonny grabbed his radio, urgently saying, "Dillon."

Dillon came back quickly. "Yeah... What's up?"

"A car just pulled up and Garcia and the other guy are climbing in. I may have to leave you for a while and follow them. I'll keep in touch and be back as soon as I can."

"Roger that. Be careful buddy."

"Will do," Sonny said, then dropped the radio on the passenger seat and started the Tahoe. As the car pulled away from the house, Sonny waited until they began to turn left at the corner. Then he put the Tahoe in gear and followed after them, staying a good distance behind.

After only two or three minutes, the car swung into the parking lot of a local bar. Sonny cruised past the bar and found a parking spot on the street about half a block down. In his rearview mirror, he saw the three men open the front door and walk in the bar. He waited a few minutes, then climbed from the Tahoe and walked to the door of the Brass Knuckles Bar. As he stepped in, he saw the threesome standing at the bar, not seeming to notice him.

He strolled around the far side and took a stool at the U-shaped bar, across and a few stools down from the trio. He hoped he was far enough away to go unnoticed, but still close enough to hear their conversation.

The bartender opened beers and set them in front of the three, then grabbed three shot glasses and poured them nearly full of tequila. *Tequila Ocho!* Sonny thought, seeing the label. *Good stuff.*

Then the bartender turned and walked his direction, saying, "What can I get'cha?"

"Got any New Castle?"

"Sure do."

"I'll have one of those," Sonny said, smiling. "One of those bags of pretzels, too," he added, pointing to the rack on the wall.

He relaxed on the bar stool, eating pretzels, sipping New Castle, and listening to the ongoing chatter from across the bar. They didn't seem to be trying to hush their conversation and, so far, we're just seeing who could out-boast the other about whose butt they had recently kicked, or what girl they were going to bed next.

There wasn't anything about the three that worried Sonny, though he could see that two of them were packing. Garcia was definitely the biggest of the three with a strong, stocky build. He wasn't sure if he was packing or not, but thought he saw signs of a shoulder holster.

The conversation changed a bit, and he heard one of the guys ask Garcia, "When you gonna head over to St. Louis?"

"Maybe Friday. I'm gonna stop by my mother's place before we go out for the evening. You want to go with us?

"Why not? Nothing going on around here right now."

Sonny slid from the barstool, saying to the bartender, "Be back in a minute. Forgot my phone in the truck."

The bartender nodded his head. "I'll save your seat for you," he said, then grinned.

In the Tahoe, Sonny grabbed the radio. "Dillon... you there?"

"Go ahead Sonny."

"I followed the three to a local bar not much more than three quarters of a mile away. I think it's better if I stay here and keep an eye on them. So, like I said, it's less than a mile... you wanna hike down here?"

Dead air on the radio for a few seconds.

Sonny keyed his radio and asked, "What'cha think?"

Still dead air.

"Dillon?"

"Sorry... a neighbor was coming down alley and had to say Hi. I'll be there in twenty minutes."

"Good. Go left at the end of the block and that'll bring you right to the bar. It's called Brass Knuckles Bar."

"Roger that," Dillon said.

Sonny put his phone in his pocket and walked back into the bar. He slid onto his barstool, took the last drink of the New Castle and held the bottle toward the bartender, who bent to grab another from his beer cooler.

Sliding it across to Sonny, the bartender asked, "More pretzels?"

"No thanks, I'm good," Sonny said lifting the New Castle. As he took another drink, he was thinking about their situation with Garcia and company. There were quite a few other men in the bar, too. Some wore leather, some wore muscle shirts, and nearly all wore lots of ink. Tats of all kinds, shapes and sizes.

And... going by the name, Brass Knuckles, it was probably a pretty tough place. It reminded Sonny of Dillon's story about his cousin who was once a big-time Heavyweight Contender who was ranked fifth in the world. The Contender was asked about the Queen of Diamonds, a bar in Northeast Minneapolis where he often hung out.

"Isn't that a pretty tough bar?" the questioner asked.

"Tough bar? I'm ranked fifth in the world as a heavyweight boxer. At the Queen of Diamonds I'm ranked thirteenth."

Sonny smiled to himself.

Chapter Sixteen

"Care for a game of cribbage?" Sonny heard from behind. He turned on his stool to see an older gentleman holding a cribbage board and a deck of cards.

His first quick thought was *No thanks,* because he didn't want to be distracted. Then he thought, *What better way to go unnoticed than two yokels playing cribbage.*

"Sure," he said. "Pull up a stool."

The older gentleman smiled, climbed onto a stool and placed the cribbage board and deck of cards on the bar. "My name's Arnie," he said, reaching out his hand.

"I'm Sonny, glad to meet you." He shook Arnie's hand and smiled, noticing a firm handshake from the lean, older gentleman.

"Not many in here know how to play cribbage. Poker's the only game they know with cards. Nice to find somebody who knows *this* game."

"Jimmy," Sonny called to the bartender to get his attention. "Get Arnie here whatever he's drinking."

As Jimmy started their direction, Arnie said, "Just a Coors Lite, Jimmy. Thanks Sonny."

Sonny reached for the deck of cards and slid them toward Arnie. "Your game, so why don't you go ahead and leadoff with dealing."

Arnie won the first game handily, and Sonny was taking a strong lead in the second game when he saw Dillon walk in the door.

Sonny looked at Dillon and gave him a subtle shake of the head. As he figured, Dillon knew that meant not to show or act like he knew Sonny. He walked around the U-shaped bar, settling on a stool four or five down from where Sonny was playing cribbage.

He ordered a beer and slowly scanned the room as he drank it. He saw Garcia and the guy from the photo drinking across from Sonny. The third guy with them must be the guy with the car. He also noticed, like Sonny had, that there were a good number of less than friendly looking guys in the place. Some playing pool, some playing music on the jukebox, some just drinking. Most looking plenty tough.

The important question was, *How many would back Garcia if they tried to take him in here?* He cringed a little and shook his head, not liking the thought.

Sonny went on to win the second game of cribbage, almost skunking Arnie. The old man grinned, saying, "That's one game each. How about one more for the championship? Loser buys the next drink?"

"You're on!" Sonny said, and pushed the deck over to Arnie for him to deal.

Just as he did that, Garcia and his buddy walked away from the bar. Sonny panic for a moment knowing he'd have to abandon Arnie in a hurry if they walked out the door. He glanced toward Dillon and noticed him watching Garcia closely, too. Then, just as quickly, Sonny's panic eased when he realized they were headed for the men's room.

When he looked back, Dillon was sliding from his stool and heading for the men's room. Rounding the corner of the bar, Dillon glanced Sonny's way, raised his eyebrows and shrugged his shoulders, trying to convey the idea that he was just checking things out.

Arnie had shuffled and dealt cards to start their third game. And, though he wasn't going to do anything just to give the game away, Sonny wanted Arnie to win so he could go away feeling good about the wonderful game of cribbage.

Garcia and friends came out of the men's room laughing, and headed back to the bar. A half minute later Dillon came out, still drying his hands on a paper towel. As he rounded the corner of the bar, he crumpled it into a ball and pitched it into a garbage bin behind the bar. He sat down and ordered another beer. His demeanor told Sonny that everything was okay.

The third game came right down to the wire. Both players were on fourth street, but luck was on Arnie's side, as both men had about sixteen holes left to peg and it was Arnie's deal. That meant it was Arnie's crib and he would have two hands against Sonny's one hand. Arnie won the game, with Sonny left in the "stink hole."

Sonny slapped Arnie on the shoulder, saying, "Great game, partner. Can't believe I left myself in the stink hole."

"That *was* a good game," Arnie said. "If we run into each other again, I'll give you a chance at revenge." The old boy gathered up his cribbage board, deck of cards and the bottle of Coors Lite Sonny bought him, then moved to the table where he'd originally been sitting. He set aside the cribbage board and began to play game of solitaire, wearing a contented grin.

Ten or fifteen minutes later, Sonny decided to take a walk to the men's room. As he passed Dillon, he gave him two quick, light taps on the back. Dillon waited about a minute, then headed for the men's room as well.

As he stepped in the men's room, Dillon immediately began glancing around, checking the room.

"We're good," Sonny said. "No one in here."

Dillon relaxed, and leaned against the door after it closed. "What'cha thinkin'."

"I'm thinkin' we're just gonna have to wait it out. These guys might be here drinkin' till who knows when."

"Yeah," Dillon said, sounding like he didn't particularly like the situation. "Don't think we should try anything here in the bar... do you?"

"Nope. Hopefully they'll head for home in a while. Meantime, why don't you go out in the truck and try to nap for about an hour, then come back and relieve me and I'll do the same."

"Are we thinkin' the same thing? Get on 'em as they're headed into their house?"

"Yup. In the house, if we have to, but preferably outside before they get to the door. Less likely to be others to interfere or get in the way."

Chapter Seventeen

"Remember that very little is needed to make a happy life."
Marcus Aurelius (121 – 180 AD)

As feared, the trio continued to drink well into the night. It was passing 1:30 in the morning, and two of the three were noticeably drunk. Garcia appeared to be a little more under control and his speech wasn't nearly as slurred. The trio talked about heading for home, and soon Garcia held out his hand to get the keys from Samson, the owner of the car who had picked them up. He handed them over to Garcia without argument.

"I was hopin' you'd ask to drive," Samson slurred.

Sonny glanced toward Dillon, who made an exaggerated effort of looking at his watch, then at the trio. Sonny nodded his head, indicating that he was ready to follow them out the door – when they did finally decide to leave the bar.

After another fifteen minutes of finishing their last drink, the trio headed for the door. Garcia helped JD get outside and to the car, where he hefted him into the back seat. He stumbled and weaved a little as he walked around to the driver's side and climbed in. The other guy, Samson, the one who's car they were using, was already comfortable in the passenger seat, head leaning back and eyes closed.

Sonny and Dillon were on the sidewalk nearing the Tahoe as Garcia and company drove past. When the vehicle went by, Sonny and Dillon hurried to the Tahoe, jumped in and pulled the doors shut.

"When they make the turn toward the house," Sonny said, "I'm going to move in on 'em fast. Grab that shotgun and be ready to jump out. I'll be right behind you."

As they neared the corner where they would turn, Sonny eased the Tahoe closer to the car. Garcia made the turn and soon was moving toward the curb to park. Sonny accelerated, swung around in front of the car and cut him off.

Before the Tahoe came to a full stop, Dillon was out and pointing the shotgun at Garcia. "Let me see your hands, Johnny!" he shouted, as he slowly circled around toward the driver's door. "Above the steering wheel!" he shouted again, even louder. "Let me see 'em, Johnny!"

Dillon's attention was focused on Garcia, and he didn't notice Samson waking up from his drunken nap. Samson wasn't sure what was happening, but he knew somebody had a shotgun pointed at his buddy, Johnny.

Grabbing his gun and pointing through the windshield at Dillon, Samson heard the loud explosion of a gunshot. Then a bullet shattered the windshield and ripped angrily through his chest. Looking down at the blood soaking his shirt, the gun fell from his hand.

Dillon glanced over quickly, and saw Sonny standing on the other side of the Tahoe, arms outstretched over the hood, gun aimed at the passenger side of the car.

"He was going to try and shoot you," Sonny shouted. "Let's get cuffs on the other two, then I'll call 9-1-1."

They heard the door of the house opening, and Sonny swung his gun that direction, yelling, "Get back inside. Now!" The door quickly slammed shut.

Soon, they had cuffs on Johnny and JD, and Sonny grabbed his phone to call for an ambulance and police. After a brief discussion, Dillon heard Sonny say, "Yes, the Jackson County Sheriff's office is aware of our efforts to bring Juan Garcia back to St. Louis." Sonny ended the call, and said, "The Sargent on duty wanted to know why we were taking someone prisoner and why we needed to shoot someone." Then, glancing toward the house, he added, "We better keep a good eye on that, too. Don't want someone coming out of there... guns blazing."

Sonny and Dillon moved Garcia and JD to the curb, with the Tahoe between themselves and the house in case anyone inside tried to get cute with a rifle, or any other gun for that matter. About four minutes later, they could hear sirens approaching

Samson's wound was taken care of and he was placed in the ambulance. He was in poor condition, but he'd make it. JD was placed under arrest and put in the back seat of the squad car.

"We'll be taking Juan Garcia back to the St. Louis County Jail in St. Louis," Sonny told the police. Then he chained Garcia to the floor of the Tahoe – handcuffs chained to the D-ring that was bolted to the back seat floor.

Leaving the scene, Sonny asked, "Wha-da-ya think? Stay the night in our room and head back tomorrow?"

"Well... I'm kind of wound up from all this. Don't know if I'd sleep. Why don't we head down the road a couple hours toward St. Louis?" Dillon said.

"Good with me. It'll probably be a couple hours before I unwind, too."

They got their stuff from the room and checked out with the night clerk. By four o'clock that morning, they were headed east toward St. Louis.

"I'm good to make it all the way, napping and trading off," Dillon said. "What do you think?"

"Let's stop and grab us a cup of coffee and a snack," Sonny said. "I can take the first shift."

Chapter Eighteen

"The best revenge is to be unlike he who performed the injury."
Marcus Aurelius (121 – 180 AD)

They turned Garcia over to officers on duty at the St. Louis County Jail at 8:45 a.m. Then, having completed all the necessary paperwork, they were headed toward the office of De Luca Bail Bonds. Sonny had reached Dominic De Luca on his phone earlier that morning, updating him since their conversation yesterday.

"We'll be turning him over to St. Louis County in about two hours and should be at your office with the paperwork around nine-thirty this morning," Sonny told him. Then, responding to a comment from De Luca about having caught the guy, he said, "And we'll be just as excited to trade you the paperwork for a check."

They spoke for another half minute or so, then, nodding his head, Sonny said, "Okay, we'll talk about it when we get to your office." He ended the call and dropped his phone in the center console of the Tahoe, where he usually kept it. He really didn't like carrying it.

"Talk about what?" Dillon asked.

"Oh, he's trying to renegotiate our fee, since we were, in his words, 'So efficient, took such a short time and didn't have any injuries on our side,' he thinks a lower fee would be fair to both sides."

Dillon shrugged, saying, "I'd maybe give him two or three percent reduction from our agreement, but not any more than that. What are you thinkin'?"

"That's exactly what I was thinking. Charging him sixteen percent instead of nineteen. Maybe fifteen if he's really pushing. We want to keep open the chance of him calling us again, too."

"I'd go along with that. It still our biggest payday ever," Dillon said, smiling broadly.

They settled on fifteen percent, with De Luca saying he'd definitely call when they had another challenging skip. Sonny slid the check into his wallet, hopped in the Tahoe, started it and pointed it northbound toward Minneapolis. Once out of the St. Louis area and traveling on open highway, Sonny dug out his phone and pressed Sonja on his speed dial.

Dillon noticed Sonny's face brighten when he heard her voice answering the phone.

"Hey Babe, how are you this morning?" he asked. Dillon listening to one side of the conversation, smiled.

"That's great!"

"Yeah, he's in the bag and we're headed for home."

"Yeah, he really is... and we really are."

"We should be there around seven-thirty, but I'm gonna crash for about twelve hours. So... I probably won't see you 'till tomorrow evening."

"You can! That's great. I'll see you at Jax at one o'clock then."

"Okay. I love you, too. Bye Babe."

Chapter Nineteen

"Perfection of character: live each day without frenzy, sloth, or pretense."
Marcus Aurelius (121 – 180 AD)

Sonny sat at a table in the barroom side of Jax, sipping Glenfiddich Scotch over one ice cube. He was about a half hour early and taking the time to decompress after the last few days. Bringing in Garcia went as good as he could've hoped for, but there'd been plenty of tense moments, including Dillon almost getting shot.

He glanced at his watch, leaned back in his chair and sipped more of the single malt whiskey. Sonja would be there in about twenty minutes. He closed his eyes, thinking about what a wonderful woman she was and how much he'd missed her these last few days.

Then his eyes brightened and a big smile crossed his face when he looked up and saw her come in the door and walk toward him. His eyes drank in her beauty, then he stood and gave her a big bear hug.

"Easy, easy big guy. You're gonna crack one of my ribs." He relaxed his arms and looked in her eyes. She smiled softly, touched his cheek with her fingertips, and said, "It's so good to see you Sonny. I missed you."

He kissed her softly, then said, "I was just thinking that same thing about you." He stepped aside and pointed to a chair. "Sit down Babe. Relax." As he moved to his chair, he waved the waiter over to their table.

"Yes... can I get you something to drink?" The waiter asked, looking at Sonja.

"Could I get a vodka gimlet, please?"

"Certainly," he said. Then, looking at Sonny, he asked, "Another for you, Sonny?"

"Sure, bring me one more."

"So, everything went well in St. Louis?" Sonja asked, getting comfortable in her chair.

"Yeah, just about as good as we could hope for. A couple of near misses... as always, but no injuries were taken on our side."

"Near misses?" Sonja asked, sounding concerned.

"Yeah, one guy tried to shoot Dillon while he was covering the guy's partner. I had to put one in him," Sonny said, then added, "Never like doing that."

She smiled softly, then reached to touch his hand.

"But..." he said, sounding brighter, "necessary evil when dealing with this element."

Sonja dealt with all kinds of jerks and low-lifes in the trucking business, but nothing like the characters in "this element" Sonny was referring to. The criminal element comes in all shapes, sizes, colors, creeds, and races... and Sonny didn't have a racist bone in his body. He had an equal opportunity dislike for all criminals. Particularly those who would do harm to others.

"Do you have anything on your calendar for the coming week?" she asked.

"No. I think I'm clean for at least a week. What would you like to do?"

"My mom headed to Tucson yesterday for the winter. Why don't we fly down and visit her for a couple days. I've got vacation time to use up before the end of the year."

"How 'bout we bring our golf clubs and go down for five or six days," Sonny said. "Maybe she'd even like to golf with us once or twice."

"How about we fly down Thursday evening and I can take Friday and all of next week off," Sonja said. "We can fly home when ever you'd like."

"Let's do it!" Sonny said. "If anything comes up, I'll just put 'em off until late next week. I think I'll spend time on my golf game this week. Go up to Edinburgh in Brooklyn Park. I love the range and practice area there. Wanna come with me a time or two?

"Sure, a couple evenings would work for me."

"How 'bout you come to my place from work. We'll start tonight, then have a bite to eat there."

"Yeah, I only have to go back in the office for about two hours," she said. "Oh, but I don't have my golf clubs."

"You can use some of mine for tonight, then throw your bag in the trunk when you get home."

"Sounds fun!" she said, raising her gimlet to toast the idea. "I'll be there by five."

Sonny smiled, hoisted his glass of scotch, then savored the flavor as he drank.

Sonja waved the waiter over, telling Sonny, "We better order some food. I'm starved."

They sat enjoying their meal and talking about the trip to Tucson, then Sonja said, "Something kinda strange happened the other day."

"What was that?" Sonny said, searching her eyes.

"Well, I had just pulled into the garage and closed the door. Then, when I stepped out the side door to go in the house, there was a guy coming up the sidewalk, saying, are you Sonja Wilkinson?

"I told him yes, and asked why he was wondering," she paused, remembering. "Then he waved an envelope at me, saying he had got a piece of my mail by mistake and was delivering it. He seemed a little creepy, so when he left I walked down the sidewalk to see where he was going. He got in a black Camaro and drove away. No big deal, but he was kinda creepy."

Sonny stared down at his glass of Glenfiddich for a few seconds, then said, "I think you should stay with me until we fly to Tucson Thursday. A guy like that, in a black Camaro, has followed me two or three times in the last couple weeks. I don't think we should take any chances."

"O-k-a-y," Sonja said slowly. "Rather than practicing tonight, you'd better meet me at my place. I'll bring things to wear the rest of this week, and pack my bag for Tucson."

"I'll be at your place at five to meet you," he said. "In fact, I'll probably get there around four o'clock and park down the block to watch your place."

"Any idea who this guy is?" Sonja asked.

"No. None at all. Dillon and I had a little run in with him on the road about a week ago. But nothing came of it."

Sonny didn't see anything of the black Camaro that afternoon, and waved to Sonja as she drove past, heading for her garage. She loaded her car with clothes, golf clubs, a suitcase and a few other odds and ends, then they headed for Northeast Minneapolis.

Sonny had an oversized double garage and kept it fairly clean so there was always room for Sonja to pull in when she came over. He'd given her an opener for the garage door, too.

When they reached his place, she pressed the button on the opener and pulled into the garage. Sonny pulled in next to her and closed the door behind them.

"Why don't we bring your things inside and put them in the guest room," he said. "No sense you hauling them around in your car all week."

"Thanks," she said, and started to grab a few things.

Later, they decided to go over to Shaws and have a burger and beer. That was another thing Sonny loved about her. She could roll with the flow and enjoy doing most anything. *Low maintenance and loves to do everything. What a woman!* he thought. He smiled a soft smile at her.

As they ate burgers and fries, and drank Grain Belt Nordeast, Sonja asked, "Why haven't you mentioned this guy before, Sonny?"

"Well, until now, I didn't want you worrying about him needlessly. No clue who he is, so when we get back from Tucson, I'll have to start digging into it a bit deeper."

"How will you start if you have no clue who he is?" she asked, seeming concerned.

"I'm not sure where I'll start, mostly hoping to catch him on the street sometime," Sonny told her. "Make him tell me who he is."

She raised her eyebrows and nodded her head thinking to herself, *I suppose. Not sure I like it, but that may be the best place to start.*

Chapter Twenty

"Be like the cliff against which the waves continually break; but stands firm and tames the fury of the water."
Marcus Aurelius (121 – 180 AD)

Sonny and Sonja took her mom, Savannah Wilkinson, grocery shopping to stock the cupboards and fridge in her Tucson home. They decided to stop at Don's Liquor Emporium to stock up on beer and wine, too.

Sonny had a phone message from Dillon, so he stepped outside and returned the call, while Sonja helped her mom put everything away. He finished the call and walked back in the kitchen, just as they were pouring two glasses of wine.

"Just in time," Sonja said. "Grab a wine glass or a beer... whichever you want."

"A beer sounds real good." He walked to the fridge and grabbed a bottle of New Castle. Then, looking around and hesitating, he asked, "Bottle opener?"

"In the drawer just to the right of the wide silverware drawer," Sonja said. "Everything okay with Dillon?"

"Yeah, he just wanted to let me know that he saw the black Camaro again. It was cruising past and slowed down in front of my home. He'll call me any time he leaves the house, so I could keep an eye on it through my phone."

"Did Dillon's brother get there to be with him at your house while we're gone?" Sonja asked, sounding concerned.

"Yeah, he got to the house a couple hours after we left. No need to worry about anything. They can handle any situation just fine."

"What's going on?" Mom asked, glancing from Sonja to Sonny. "Doesn't sound very good."

"Not quite sure, yet," Sonny said. "There's a guy that's been following me and we've seen his car twice at my place and once at Sonja's."

"Once at Sonja's..." her mom started to say, angrily. Then she stopped, tried to compose herself, and said, "You know my feelings about your work Sonny, and the criminal element you deal with every day. So I won't start in on that again. I just hope you both know what you're doing when it comes to a wacko like this."

"Yes, Sonny is always a step ahead of any wacko," Sonja said, "and he's always overly-protective of me. But, thank you for your concern." She got out of her chair, stepped over and hugged her mom.

"Well... okay then," mom said. "I'll try to stay out of it and just enjoy our time together."

Sonny walked over to her and reached out his arms. She stood and hugged him. "Thank you, Savannah," Sonny said. "I'm sure it's very difficult to believe your daughter is safe in the midst of the kind of people I deal with. But she *is* and always will be. You don't have to worry."

"I believe you and I trust you," she said, stepping back and squeezing his hands. "But it's very hard for a mother not to be concerned." Then, trying to lighten the mood, she reached for her glass and raised it up, saying, "Especially when you're wine glass is empty."

"Well, we better take care of that," Sonja said, smiling.

Saturday afternoon Sonny had a call from Dillon, saying he and his brother were going out for the evening. "For dinner and a few beers, so we might not get home until one or two in the morning. I wanted to give you heads up to check security on your phone tonight... just in case. "

"Thanks for calling," Sonny said. "We planned on relaxing at home this evening anyway. Twenty-seven holes of golf can wear me out now days."

"Poor guy. I feel so bad for you."

"I know, I know. Thanks for the sympathy. Keep your cell phone on, though, in case I have to call you."

"Will do," Dillon said. "Talk to you tomorrow."

Sonny hung up his phone, and answered Sonja's questioning expression. "Dillon wanted me to know that they were going out tonight, and to watch things on my phone."

Satisfied with the explanation, she returned to their golf scorecard to finish tallying the scores. "Aha!" She exclaimed. "I won the last nine forty-three to forty-four. So, with the shots you have to give me, you won the first nine, and I won the second and third nine, and the overall total!"

"So, how much do I owe you? Less than a thousand I hope."

"How quickly you forget. The loser cooks dinner tonight. Put your chef's hat on, Mr. Loser!"

"Peanut butter sandwiches for supper... sounds good to me," Sonny said, then ducked Sonja's swing.

"Oh no you don't... steaks, medium rare," she insisted.

That evening, the three of them enjoyed thick, juicy ribeye steaks – medium rare. Savannah had to cover her mouth to keep from laughing and spitting out the food she was chewing, when Sonja said, "Great job on grilling the ribeyes... Mr. Loser!" Heavy emphasis on the *Mr. Loser.*

Sonny glanced at both women. He could only shrug and smile, sheepishly. Then he picked up his glass and sipped his favorite scotch – Glenfiddich – poured over a single ice cube.

Chapter Twenty-One

*"Very little is needed to make a happy life;
it is all within your way of thinking."*
Marcus Aurelius (121 – 180 AD)

When they'd finished dinner, and Sonny had cleaned up the kitchen – further penance for losing that afternoon – they decided to watch "Last of the Dogmen," one of Sonny's favorite movies that he'd brought with on DVD.

About midway through the movie, Sonny was glancing at the home security system on his phone. Suddenly, he sat upright and reached for the remote of the DVD player. He pressed the *Pause* button and dropped the remote on the couch next to where he sat.

He got to his feet, trying to remember how to operate the security system from his phone. "Come on... come on," he said, sounding frustrated. Finally, he hit the right button and the floodlights on his home and garage lit up his whole yard in Northeast Minneapolis.

Then, pressing another button, he began shouting at the phone. "What the hell you think you're doin' out there, prowlin' around my place? Better get gone in a big hurry, or get to duckin' bullets."

The guy – who'd been peeking around the garage, then sneaking across the yard toward the house – turned, ran back to his vehicle and took off, tires squeeling. *The same black Camaro*, Sonny thought.

"It worked!" he exclaimed. "Scared the beejeebers out of the guy and he hightailed it outta there."

"Wow," Savannah said, "How'd you do that? Made it sound like you were inside the house. Works pretty slick, whatever it is."

"New security system he *finally* had installed," Sonja said, showing a little smugness.

"With six inches of new snow covering everything, it really lit up the place," Sonny said. "I better give Dillon a call. Let him know to be a little careful when he goes home tonight." He let Dillon know what had happened that evening, then said, "When I'm back home next week, we're gonna get on this SOB's trail and figure out who he is."

"Sounds good to me. The guy's becoming a real pain in the arse."

"We'll be landing early on Friday afternoon," Sonny told him. "See you at my place later that afternoon." He ended the call and pressed the app for his security system. Soon he had all six cameras from home showing on his telephone screen again. He turned the phone for the other two to see, saying, "The wonderful world of technology. Ain't it grand!"

Sonja looked at her mom, shrugged and said softly, "Been tryin' to convince him of that for two years now."

Savannah just smiled and sipped her wine.

Sonny walked over, plopped back down on the couch and punched *Play* on the remote. As the movie began again, Sonja said, "You're right my love, this movie is great."

Chapter Twenty-Two

"Because a thing seems difficult for you, do not think it impossible for anyone to accomplish."
Marcus Aurelius (121 – 180 AD)

After landing in Minneapolis the following Friday, they stood waiting for their suitcases and golf bags to show up on the carousel. Sonja said, "Okay, but just this next week, then I'm moving back home."

"Hopefully, we'll have a lead on the wacko by then and I won't be worrying so much about you being alone at your home."

"Did you invite Dillon to dinner?" she asked.

"Yup. He'd like to go over to Mancini's. Said his uncle is playing in the band there tonight."

"Fine by me. I love Mancini's," she said, pointing to a suitcase coming down the conveyor belt.

At half past seven that evening, four of them sat at a table in the barroom of Mancini's – Sonja, Sonny, Dillon, and Dillon's girlfriend Vicki Bissett. They were enjoying drinks, talking of the week in Tucson, and hearing Sonny moan about his poor golf game.

"Just admit it, Sonny," Dillon said, making it sound like common knowledge. "You're never happy with your golf game... no matter what you shoot."

"Well... there is that!" Sonny said, then broke into laughter at himself.

"Yes... there is that," Sonja said.

They ate a delicious dinner, each having a T-bone steak, and were relaxing with after dinner drinks and enjoying the music of the band. Between songs, Sonny asked, "Seen anything more of the stranger in the black Camaro?"

"No, none at all," Dillon said, leaning forward with his elbows on the table. "We had a little fresh snow, and there haven't been any new tire tracks or footprints since you turned the security system loose on him."

"I'm not sure where we'll start, but we've got to get a line on this guy, now that he's involved Sonja. I've asked her to stay with me this week, but she insists that she is going back home when the week is up."

"Okay then," Dillon said, smiling at Sonja, "we've got a deadline to meet."

At one o'clock Saturday afternoon, Sonny and Sonja were sharing a light lunch of clam chowder and crackers, when his cell phone rang. He pulled it from his pocket, looked at the screen, and said, "It's Saul Berkowitz, wonder what he's up to on a Saturday?"

"Saul Berkowitz!" he said brightly, as he answered the phone. "How are you old friend?" He smiled softly at Sonja, as he listened to Saul's conversation.

"Yes, we just got back yesterday afternoon from Tucson, visiting Sonja's mom."

"Sure. It would be our pleasure to join you," he said, then looked apologetically at Sonja for not asking her first. "We'll be there at two thirty tomorrow afternoon."

He listened a little more, then said, "Sounds great, Saul. See you tomorrow."

He shut his phone off and slid it on the table, as Sonja gave him a big smile. "Where are we going to be at two-thirty tomorrow?"

"Saul and Ester's home. They're having a little get-together with a few family and people from the office. He's grilling lamb chops. I've had them and they're to die for."

"It does sound like fun. I've never been to their home."

"They're up on the hill in St. Anthony," Sonny said, "near Stinson and St. Anthony Pkwy. Very nice home with a beautiful back yard. You'll love it!"

Sonja was certain she would enjoy the get-together with Saul and Ester, and fall in love with their home. She never questioned Sonny's taste – in things or in people – especially in people. She knew him to be an excellent judge of character... always.

And, again, Sonny was right. She adored Ester and Saul, fell in love with their home and back yard – there was a light snow falling to add ambience – and she just had to know how Saul seasoned and grilled his lamb chops so that they were, "... so absolutely mouthwatering!"

The day was perfect. Everything was perfect. Until... she heard her phone buzz inside her purse. She had no intention of answering it, but reached in to glance at the screen to see who was calling. "It's from Home Safe," she said, almost whispering to Sonny. "I better get it," she continued softly. "Might be trouble."

She grabbed her phone, rose from her chair, and said, "Excuse me. I'm so sorry. It might be an emergency, so I'd better take this call." She walked down the hallway toward the bathroom, saying, "Hello, this is Sonja Wilkinson."

She slowed, listening carefully, then said, "Okay. Thank you for calling. Tell the police I should be there in twenty-five or thirty minutes."

She hurried back to the table, grabbed her purse, and said, "I'm so very sorry, but we have to leave immediately. Someone's broken into my home and set off the alarm. I have to get there to meet with the police right away. Thank you so much, Ester and Saul. It was such a wonderful time. I hope we can get together again, soon."

Sonny shook Saul's hand, gave Ester a big hug and quickly thanked them both. Saul shooed them away, saying, "Go... now... drive safely."

Chapter Twenty-Three

"Though you break your heart, life will go on just as before."
Marcus Aurelius (121 – 180 AD)

At her home in Eagan, Sonja sat talking to the local police officers, as Sonny was checking everything for his own satisfaction. She told them the story of a guy stopping with a piece of her mail, claiming it had come in his mail by mistake and he was just returning it.

"I was a little suspicious of him the whole time. The way he talked? The way he acted? I'm not exactly sure why. My memory of him is a little vague, and all I remember for sure is that he left in a black Camaro."

One of the officers asked if she could give a description to a sketch artist. "I think so," she said, with a shrug. "Enough that it might be of some help any way."

"Can you stop in the morning before you go in to work?" the officer asked.

"I've got an important meeting that'll take most of the morning. How about after lunch... 1:30?"

"That would be great. They can scan it and get it to us as soon as you're finished," the officer said. "And send it out to every department in the area, for that matter."

Before the Eagan Police officers left, Sonny relayed the episodes of being followed several times by a black Camaro. "I don't think it's a coincidence that the guy here was driving a black Camaro. Following me and coming to Sonja's home?"

"No," the officer that Sonny thought was in charge said, "it doesn't sound like it. We'll put a BOLO out on the black Camaro. See what we come up with." He handed Sonny a business card. "Call me when you get back home and leave a message with that license number you said you had jotted down on your desk blotter."

Sonny nodded. "You got it."

*　　*　　*

On Monday morning, Sonny and Dillon were having breakfast at Hazel's, their favorite place for breakfast. Sonny had with him his two Uniden hand-held police scanners. They were two years old, but still among the best scanners available on the market. Sonny handed one to Dillon, saying, "Didn't know when we'd get to use these again."

"Let's keep an ear tuned for anything on the BOLO," Dillon said. "You know the police aren't going to tell us a thing about this character. If we want any hope of getting to him and putting the fear of God in him about staying away from Sonja, then where gonna have to intercept something and find out where he's at."

"I know. And I do want to put the fear of God in him... a real strong fear."

As they finished breakfast, Sonny said, "Stop by the house for a minute, would ya? I had a message this morning from Murray Blum over at A-1 Bail Bonds." He stood from his chair, finished wiping his mouth with his napkin and tossed it on the table. "Maybe he's got a good job for us this week."

Back in his office, Sonny dialed the number for A-1 Bail Bonds, and heard, "Good morning, this is A-1 Bail Bonds. How can I help you?"

"Hi. Can I speak to Murray?"

"May I tell him who is calling, please?

"This is Sonny Sawyer. I'm returning his call."

"Thank you, Mr. Sawyer. It'll be just one moment, please."

Sonny leaned back in his desk chair, hoping Murray had a skip that needed tracing. He signaled for Dillon to sit down and relax. After about a half of minute of "easy listening music," he heard, "Hello Sonny, this is Murray. How are you?"

"Been great Murray. Busy, but that's great too."

"How's this week lookin', Sonny? I've got a hot one."

"This week is mostly open. What'cha got?"

"Well... I got a bruiser that put my regular guy in the hospital. Thought we were going to have the skip back in court last week, but it didn't work out. Only got three weeks left on the bond. But I'm pretty sure where to find him, so it's mostly getting him under control and delivered to jail."

"Sounds like I'll need my partner, Dillon, so I'll have to charge you the nineteen percent for risky ones, plus unusuals. I can be over and get a copy of your file in about an hour, if that works for you."

"Make it eleven o'clock. That'll give me a little more time to have someone copy the whole file. See you then."

Sonny hung up his phone, then stared at Dillon for a moment. He grinned slightly, closed his eyes, and slowly shook his head. "Things just keep falling into place. Murray's got a two hundred thousand dollar bond on a guy that put his regular agent in the hospital. He's gonna pay us the nineteen percent plus unusuals. What're you gonna do with all these big paydays... all this big money?"

Dillon laughed. "Save it for the rainy days... like always."

Chapter Twenty-Four

"The sorrow anger produces is far more harmful
than the thing which angered you."
Marcus Aurelius (121 – 180 AD)

At ten minutes to eleven, they were at the offices of A-1 Bail Bonds – Dillon's usual insistence that they be early for any appointment. They sat in the reception area, waiting for Murray Blum. The receptionist told them he would be returning from the courthouse by eleven o'clock, "... for your appointment."

"That's okay," Sonny said. "We're a little early anyway." She didn't notice Sonny giving the evil eye look to Dillon. Nor did she notice Dillon's big grin.

In minutes, they were in Murray's office discussing his file on the skip, Ben Morgan. "His ex-wife and their two sons live in Shakopee," Murray told them. "He tries to spend as much time there as he can. According to her, they get along better now than when they were married. She knows he's probably going away for a couple years this time, but she says he's good to the boys. So...."

"He hasn't ever left the state, or gone on the run?" Dillon asked.

Murray stared out his office window. "No, he thinks he can stay around to be with them, and just keep dodging us. We've caught him twice now, with surveillance on her house. First time, he just plain got away from our guy. Second time, he left our guy unconscious in the street, with two broken bones in his hand."

"I don't think the guy will be leaving me or Dillon unconscious in the street," Sonny said. "Nor will he just plain get away. If we can locate him that easily, we'll have him in the Hennepin County Jail in a short while."

"Okay, but I should let you know that he sometimes has one or two guys with him," Murray said. "And they're all pretty good size, rough characters."

"No problem, Mr. Blum," Dillon said, with no sign of boasting or overconfidence in his voice. "We'll take care of it for you."

"That's good to know," Blum said. "I hope to hear he's locked up in the coming days." He stood and extended his hand, shaking theirs and thanking them.

They headed back toward Sonny's home, and Dillon asked, "When do you want to start a stakeout on her home?"

"I'm open tomorrow afternoon," Sonny said. "How 'bout you?" It came up in their meeting with Murray that, with the boys in school, Morgan usually comes around in the late afternoon or early evening.

"Sounds good to me," Dillon said.

"Why don't we leave my house at two o'clock. We can be set up by three that way, before the boys get off the bus from school."

Dillon was rubbing his hands together, looking eager to get started. "I'll be there at ten minutes to...."

"I know you will," Sonny said, smiling. "Our stakeout should be fairly easy with no recognition of the new faces, new vehicle, new routine. Hopefully he lets his guard down."

The next day, it was ten minutes past three when they had set up surveillance on Mrs. Morgan's home. Her home was situated near the middle of the block, so they parked in the shade of a large oak tree near the corner of Eighth Avenue and Connor Street. Mrs. Morgan's was about three houses down the street from them. They had a good view of the home's front door, side door, driveway and garage.

"Ben Morgan is supposed to be driving a dark blue, 2005 Saturn Kia," Dillon said, looking from the file to Sonny.

"Yup... if he's not riding with one of his goons."

"Yeah, I suppose we'll just have to go by the photos of them in that case."

Sonny peeled a banana and watched out the window.

"That looks pretty good," Dillon said, reaching in the cooler and bringing out one for himself.

At three-thirty-five, the school bus stopped at the intersection directly behind them. The two Morgan boys and three other students got off the bus. As they walked by, one of the Morgan boys asked, "Need help finding something?"

Sonny quickly grabbed the closed file that lay on the console and waved it in the air. "Nope. Just a Realtor showing my clients some homes this afternoon. We've got a few to look at around the neighborhood, so we're just gonna probably leave the vehicle here and walk around. It's such a beautiful day, today."

"Okay. Good luck," the boy said and moved on.

"Thanks," Sonny shouted out the window. "And thanks for offering to help."

"Hope that doesn't blow our cover," Dillon said.

"I don't think so. Who pays attention to Realtors showing homes in the neighborhood?"

"Well, there is that, I guess."

That evening, Mrs. Morgan had no visitors. None of the male variety anyway. Only one neighbor lady that went in for about a half hour visit. At midnight, after all the lights in the house had been off for more than a half hour, they decided to pack it in and head for home.

"Same time tomorrow?" Sonny asked, as they pulled in his driveway.

Dillon was looking at the calendar on his phone, and suddenly said, "Oh man! I forgot all about my dentist appointment. It's tomorrow afternoon at three o'clock."

"Getting those two wisdom teeth pulled?"

"Yeah, but I can reschedule it in the morning."

"No. Don't do that," Sonny said. "I'll be fine out there tomorrow. I'll keep in touch if anything happens. I'll see you Friday afternoon, and we'll probably have to work long days Saturday and Sunday."

"Okay. Two o'clock Friday then," Dillon said, sounding a little disappointed.

"See you at ten minutes to...," Sonny said, smiling.

Thursday afternoon, Sonny went down early, had a burger for lunch at the Lion's Tap, then headed over to Mrs. Morgan's home. In the back of his mind, he almost hoped that he wouldn't see anyone again today.

His concern was partly so Dillon wouldn't feel bad about not being here, and partly because Morgan could show up with one or two of his thugs, which might become very unpleasant. Not that he had any concern about being able to handle it, but with Dillon there to team up, it would likely be much less of a problem.

Soon, the school bus stopped behind him and the same group of kids got off. As they walk by, the Morgan boy, who had offered help yesterday, said, "No customer today?"

Sonny smiled and said, "He had to pick up his wife at work today. They'll be here pretty soon."

"Okay," the boy said, waving to Sonny as he hurried to catch up with his brother.

Sonny munched on apples and bananas that afternoon, and ate an onion and liverwurst sandwich for supper. He drank Mountain Dew. He liked it, but it was mostly for the caffeine to help keep him alert.

At about half past six, a blue Subaru SUV drove by and swung into Mrs. Morgan's driveway. Two men got out, and Sonny was certain that the driver was Ben Morgan. He didn't recognize the other man from any of the photos. He watched as Mrs. Morgan open the screen door and invited the two into her home.

Sonny thought about how he would take Ben Morgan into custody. He had the M11, which could knock both of the men down and incapacitate them briefly. And he'd faced two tough men more than a few times as a skip tracer. As he's thinking about this, he reached for his phone and punched in Dillon's number. *He should be home from the dentist by now,* he thought.

On the third ring, he heard, "Hey Big Guy. How's it going?"

"Going good. How'd things go at the dentist?"

"Good. Pulled both wisdom teeth without a problem. Went home and tried to rest, but I couldn't sleep, so I'm headed your way. Be there in about fifteen minutes."

"That's great. Ben Morgan is here... with one of his thugs. Thought I was going to have to do battle alone. But I'll hold off 'til you get here, or as long as I can."

"Okay. How about I park on the other end of the block? So they don't see there are two of us right away."

"Good idea. I'll watch for you. Fire up your two-way radio on channel 11."

"Got it."

Sonny sat back, a little more at ease knowing he didn't have to battle both of them on his own. He reached down and turned up the volume of the Lefty Frizzell CD that was in his player. He turned the volume up until he could hear it, but just barely. "I Never Go around Mirrors" was playing, a great country classic, and one of Sonny's favorites.

Sonny sat relaxing, listening to Lefty, and watching the Morgan house, when suddenly the screen door swung opened and out came Morgan and his buddy. They walked up the driveway briskly, confidently, with purpose. They turned up the street and headed toward Sonny's Tahoe.

Chapter Nineteen

"It is not death that a man should fear,
but instead fear never beginning to really live."
Marcus Aurelius (121 – 180 AD)

Sonny quickly assessed the situation, and decided to meet them outside the vehicle, ready for trouble. He opened the door, slid out and quietly shut the door. He walked a little ways toward the two, then stopped and waited.

"What's yer name, buddy?" Morgan shouted.

"Who's asking?" Sonny answered, further assessing his situation. Both men were smaller than he. Shorter by two inches and lighter by maybe twenty pounds. Sizable men nonetheless. And rugged looking.

The two continued toward him, coming faster. Sonny started backing away from them. Then, just as they closed in on him, he bent and charged through the two, much like his days playing tight end in Division II college football. This caught them off guard and knocked them sideways a bit, causing both to struggle in catching their balance.

In an instant, Sonny planted his foot, turned, and sent a huge right fist toward Morgan's head. It hit home – the full force of his two hundred thirty pounds behind it. It landed hard on Morgan's ear, snapping his head violently sideways. He knew then he wouldn't need to be concerned with him for a bit. He'd learned long ago that the human brain is *much* more sensitive, and susceptible, to trauma in a hard sideways collision, than it is in a front-to-back collision.

A solid blow to the side of a man's head will usually leave him disoriented, dizzy, feeling sick, and not ready to get right back into any fight.

The other guy was quickly returning his attention to Sonny, having been stunned momentarily by his quick move between them, then by his partner slumping to his knees in a dazed condition. He turned and swung a big left hook toward Sonny, who deflected it away with his own left, then lunged in close and threw his right elbow hard into the man's throat, nearly knocking him off his feet.

The guy was gasping for air, then he felt Sonny's foot kick him hard on the side of his knee. The pain from his knee screamed in his head, and set fireworks flashing behind his closed eye lids.

Sonny wasn't sure if the guy was able to fight anymore, so — not taking any chances — he threw a left into the side of the man's head snapping it violently to the side, much the same as his slumping partner had experienced, having much the same result. With both of them dazed, Sonny grabbed the handcuffs clipped to the back of his belt and cuffed Morgan's hands behind his back. Then he ran to the Tahoe, grabbed another pair from the center console and cuffed the other guy, who began shouting at him a bit incoherently, evidently still in a dazed condition.

He walked back to the Tahoe, retrieved his radio from the passenger seat, keyed it, and said, "Dillon, you there?"

"Go ahead."

"Where you at?"

"About a minute away. Need something?"

"Nope. Come on down to my end. I got Morgan and his crony in cuffs."

"Really? I'll be there in two shakes."

In less than a minute, Dillon turned the corner at the far end of the block and drove up, parking nose-to-nose with the Tahoe. He slid from behind the wheel, walked around his car, and said, "What the hell happened here?" He crossed his arms and smiled, as he looked from the two on the ground to Sonny, who was rubbing sore knuckles.

"They came at me with plans to kick my butt. I think I spoiled their plans."

"I think you did," Dillon said, laughing as he tried to get the words out.

They spent the next few minutes switching the handcuffs on the two thugs. Switching them from hands behind their backs, to hands in front. Then they loaded them into the back seat of the Tahoe, and chained the cuffs to the D-ring bolted to the floor.

"I turned on my video camera and set it on the dash, before I got out of the Tahoe. Hopefully I'll have evidence of assault on this other moron," Sonny said, reaching in to grab the camera and turn it off.

"Good move, Buddy. There's hope for you yet... for you and the wonderful world of technology."

"I'm gonna call Murray Blum and let him know we'll be bringing Morgan to the Hennepin County Jail in about an hour," Sonny said, reaching in the center console for his phone. "I'm sure Murray will be headed home, so we'll bring the paperwork over in the morning and get our check."

"I don't feel like I earned my usual split," Dillon said, sounding apologetic.

"*BALONEY*," Sonny said, emphatically. "You know that we're always in this together... no matter what."

Dillon held out his hand. "Thanks," he said, as Sonny grabbed his hand and shook it firmly.

Chapter Twenty-Six

"A wrongdoer can be one who has left something undone,
not always one who has done something wrong."
Marcus Aurelius (121 – 180 AD)

After dropping off the paperwork on Ben Morgan, and picking up a check from Murray Blum, Dillon and Sonny headed up to Hazel's Diner for breakfast. From there they went to Sonny's home, with plans to spend the whole day – the whole weekend if need be – going through boxes of old files on skips they'd traced and brought to justice. Dillon sometimes wondered about Sonny's meticulous system with a file on every skip, the vast majority of which they had indeed brought to justice, and only a very few of which – two to be exact – managed to slip through their fingers.

"This isn't the only reason to keep files," Sonny said, as they sat in his office beginning the tedious task of sorting through nearly eight years' worth of files, "but it's as good a reason as any."

They were searching for a needle in this haystack of files. Finding that "needle," was finding the someone with reason enough to come after Sonny. Someone with a vendetta. Someone with a particular dislike. Someone willing to try and take Sonny down. It would be no easy task finding that particular someone.

"I'm thinking it would have to be somebody who ended up with a long prison sentence, or maybe their friend or relative ended up with a long stretch," Sonny said. "Then again, maybe just someone with a burning hatred – and how do we measure that searching through files?"

Dillon gave him a sideways, questioning look. Sonny just grinned and returned his attention to the file he was currently paging through. Then, thinking out loud, he said, "Maybe someone will jump out at us... a little different from the rest for some weird reason."

"R-i-i-ght!" Dillon said slowly, sarcastically. Then he grabbed another file and began scanning the pages. File after file, they read on through the day; jotting notes and asking each other questions about a particular skip, or their family and friends.

"Do you remember this guy, Jackson Blake?" Dillon asked, tapping the file he held. "He and his brother thought they were going to be big time bank robbers."

"Yeah, I remember them. They both ended up doing a five to seven in Stillwater, didn't they?"

"Your memory's good. Question is... do they have anybody on the outside that might have a serious dislike for you on their behalf?"

"No, I don't think so," Sonny said, pausing in thought. "I remember their dad, when I talked to him after the trial, was just thankful we hadn't shot either of them. 'Not that they didn't deserve it,' he'd said."

Dillon nodded, closed the file, dropped it in the box and grabbed the next one. The two of them looked through file after file, until they had eliminated four of the eleven storage boxes filled with files that were stored in chronological order by the date the case was completed and they were paid.

Sonny glanced at the clock. "Is it really five-fifteen already?"

"You know what they say about time flying and having fun," Dillon said, grinning.

Trying to ignore the comment, Sonny stood, stretched, and said, "Sonja should be home from work any time now. You and Vicki have any plans for dinner?"

"Not yet."

"Give her a call and see if you'd like to join us about six-thirty. Sonja wanted to go to Emily's this evening. I know that you and Vicki love the food there."

"I think you can count on it, but I better give her a call to be sure she hasn't made other plans," Dillon said, reaching in his pocket for his phone. He dialed Vicki's number and asked her about joining Sonny and Sonja and Emily's this evening.

"Six-thirty or so," he said, answering her question.

"That's great, I was hoping you'd be up for it."

"That's okay. I'll be at your place at six-thirty, and we'll get there as quick as we can."

"Love you, too. See you at six-thirty."

Slipping his phone back in his pocket, he told Sonny, "We'll meet you there, probably a few minutes late. Need to give Vic the time to get home from work, cleanup and get ready."

"Maybe we should meet at Jax first, have a drink or two, then head to Emily's," Sonny said.

"Good idea! I'm sure Vic won't object to that. We'll meet you there."

Later that evening, they sat at a table in Emily's enjoying a delicious Lebanese dinner. Sonja and Sonny were having their usual, which was the Lebanese salad with feta cheese, raw kibbi, and cabbage rolls all covered with garlic dressing. Most eat raw kibbi with olive oil poured over it. Sonny and Sonja enjoy it more covered with the thick, delicious garlic dressing.

Vic ordered Lamb Shish Kabob, and Dillon had the Combination Dinner that included portions of baked and raw kibbi, cabbage rolls, stuffed grape leaves, meat pie, and stuffed zucchini.

"Emily's Lebanese Delicatessen..." Sonny said, raising his Pepsi in salute. "It just doesn't get any better."

Chapter Twenty-Seven

"Receive prosperity without arrogance; always ready to let it go."
Marcus Aurelius (121 – 180 AD)

Saturday morning, Dillon was at Sonny's to spend another day looking through files for that "needle in the file stack." So far, they had found three different possibilities as the someone who might be out to get Sonny. But, with each one, they ruled out the person as they discussed the various aspects of them and their case.

They were nearly halfway through the boxes, and hoped to finish the job that evening. "Vikes are playing the Packers tomorrow at noon," Sonny said. "I don't want to still be looking at files when the game starts."

"No argument from me," Dillon said. "Let's just hope we can figure out who this guy is."

They were sitting in Sonny's office, Sonny in his desk chair and Dillon on the floor leaning against the wall. Taking the next file, Dillon said, "Oh boy! Here's my old friend Dave Lyons. He's the one that blindsided me with a piece of two by four, and put my lights out.

"Yeah, I remember that one," Sonny said, a little embarrassed because he was chuckling about the incident. "I was surprised you came out of it as quick as you did. I was sure you'd be laid up for a couple weeks with a serious concussion. You were back in action and feeling good two days later."

"That's right... but only after you made me go see the doctor and get his approval."

127

"W-e-l-l," Sonny said slowly, "we all, especially Vic, wanted to be sure you didn't have a serious concussion. As far as Lyons being our suspect, I think he would have a bigger grudge against *you*, the way you worked him over before he got the chance to blindside you."

"Yer probably right," Dillon said, staring at the file he held and slowly dropping it in the box. Then he grabbed the next one from the stack.

Several hours passed before they found another suspect. Sonny was reading the file on Jake Gabovitch, a drug dealer that took almost five weeks to trace and apprehend. They had chased him through Minneapolis, Duluth, the Quad Cities area, then Chicago – even though bounty hunting is not legal in Illinois – and back to St. Paul, where they finally put the cuffs on him and brought him to the Hennepin County Jail.

"I think Gabovitch is doing a long stint in Stillwater, otherwise he's a possibility," Sonny said, looking at Dillon.

"Yeah, he was a nasty one, and he seriously threatened you a few times."

"He threatened to kill me five times, including the time in the courtroom when they pronounce him guilty."

"Think he could have anyone on the outside doing his bidding for him?" Dillon asked.

"Could be... could have one of his old crew that's still loyal to him. Stick his picture on the board behind you? I nominate him as 'Most Wanted' – for now any way."

Dillon got up from the floor, took Gabovitch's photo and pinned it to Sonny's bulletin board.

Sonny set the Gabovitch file to the side of his desk and reached for the next one. They were each becoming more adept at quickly scanning files and eliminating the people. By four o'clock that afternoon, they were starting on box ten of eleven, and optimistic about completing the project in time to take Sonja and Vic to a late dinner at Jax.

Starting on the eleventh and last box, Sonny grabbed the file of George "Bulldog" Jackson. His rap sheet had been fairly extensive already, when he skipped bail on an aggravated robbery charge. Saul Berkowitz had hired them to bring him in. Sonny and Dillon agreed that the nickname of "Bulldog" was right on. He was short and thick – about 5' 7", 230 pounds – and a tough, mean scrapper in fights.

They had found Jackson by way of his pet bulldog "Zeus." George wasn't thinking much, always hauling Zeus around with him in his pickup truck and forgetting there was a tracking devise. When Zeus was a puppy, he had a GPS chip implanted under the puppy's skin. George was a little paranoid – sure someone was going to steal his new puppy.

Sonny had seen a note regarding the chip implant in an early police report on a possible theft of Zeus. He tracked down the Veterinarian who had implanted the chip, and, with a warrant from the Hennepin County Sheriff's office, got the necessary information to track Zeus. It led them to a place owned by a friend of George's, that was about five miles northwest of Twig, Minnesota – a tiny town about a half hour northwest of Duluth. The friend's place was basically self-sufficient and "off-the-grid."

Sonny and Dillon set up surveillance in the woods about halfway between the road and the house. The first day was not productive.

Mid-morning on the second day, they saw George taking Zeus for a walk. Then they heard him shout to his friend inside the house, "Need anything else from the store?"

The words were muffled from inside the house, but evidently the friend had told him he didn't need anything else. Sonny told Dillon in a loud whisper, "I'm going to block the driveway with the Tahoe. You be ready to take George when he gets out to see what's going on."

Dillon gave him the thumbs up, and said, "I'll be there," as Sonny ran toward the Tahoe.

Jackson and Zeus roared down the driveway in his old pickup. Soon, Jackson was cussing and stomping on the brake pedal when he saw that his way was blocked. He slammed the gear shift into park, jumped out of the truck, and came at the Tahoe cussing and ready for a fight.

"What in hell you think yer doin' blockin' our driveway like you are? Get that piece of...." George stopped his shouting mid-sentence, when he heard the slide of a shotgun jack a shell into the chamber. He froze, then slowly turned and saw Dillon holding Sonny's sawed-off shotgun with a pistol grip. It was pointed directly at Bulldog's chest.

"O-h-h-h," Bulldog said slowly. "Big man! Tough guy with a shotgun in your hands."

Dillon jacked the shells from the shotgun and looked up at Sonny, saying, "Hold this for me, would ya?"

Sonny slid from the Tahoe and walked toward Dillon, who heaved it through the air to him. Then, raising his empty hands and looking at Bulldog, "There you go. No shotgun in my hands. No gun at all."

Bulldog saw this as his opening and instantly moved to take advantage of it. In two big, quick steps he was near enough to Dillon to throw a right hand haymaker. Dillon quickly leaned back and to his left, feeling only the rush of air from the punch flying past his face. Bulldog quickly came back with a left hook, aimed at the side of Dillon's head. Dillon immediately tucked his head and left shoulder toward his right knee slipping under the hook.

Missing with the left hook, Bulldog left his side wide open. Dillon threw a hard right into Bulldog's kidney, a quick left into his gut, and the third shot – another hard right to the kidney – was enough to drop him to his knees, his back cramped up in pain from the pile drivers to his kidney.

Sonny moved quickly to handcuff Jackson, saying, "We're taking you back to the Hennepin County Jail to await your hearing on the aggravated assault charge." He and Dillon each grabbed an arm and hoisted Jackson to his feet, putting him in the back seat of the Tahoe and chaining him to the D-ring, as usual.

Staring blankly at the file and thinking back, Sonny said, "He was an ornery one, alright."

Dillon was staring at the ceiling and thinking back. "He was tough as nails, but not quite the fighter he figured himself to be."

"Yeah, but he was a scrapper and fearless... you have to give him that. And he was a loner, except for his friend up in Twig. According to the notes in the file, George still has two years left up in Sandstone. And I don't think we'd need to worry about that weaselly little guy from Twig." Sonny dropped the file in the box and grabbed the next one on the stack. Dillon returned to the file he'd been scanning.

At six-thirty Saturday evening, Dillon called Vicki to let her know they'd be done with the file project, cleaned up and ready to pick her up for dinner at eight o'clock. Sonny walked to the den and told Sonja the same.

"I'll be ready and waiting," she said, and kissed him on the cheek.

Chapter Twenty-Eight

"I always look for the best; always prepared for the opposite."
Marcus Aurelius (121 – 180 AD)

At half past eight, Sonny turned the Tahoe into Jax parking lot along University Avenue. As the four of them walked toward the restaurant, Dillon tapped Sonny's arm and pointed behind them and toward University Avenue. Sonny glanced back and saw the black Camaro parked along the curb, headlights on and engine still running.

"Let's take the girls inside, and get our table. You and I can go out the back and circle around on him if he's still there," Sonny said, softly.

"Circle around on who?" Sonja said, starting to look back behind them.

Sonny caught her quickly, saying, "Don't look back. It's that black Camaro and we're hoping he doesn't know we've seen him."

Dillon saw the questioning look on Vicki's face, and quickly said, "I'll explain inside."

They walked in the front door of Jax and were seated at a table in the restaurant. "We're going to go out the back to check on this guy in the black Camaro," Sonny told them. "Be back in a few minutes. Order drinks for us, please."

They hurried through the patio area and circled around, trying to come up on the Camaro from the backside. They snuck through the yard of the home north of the parking lot and spotted the Camaro still parked at curb.

"You take the sidewalk side. I'll go around to the driver side," Sonny said, hurrying toward the car.

As they neared the Camaro, guns drawn, they realized no one was in the car. Sonny tried the handle on the driver's door, but it was locked. The same was true for Dillon on the passenger door.

They looked at each other, both wondering. Sonny quietly said, "Let's go check the Tahoe." They moved quickly toward the parking lot, but soon could see that there was no one around Sonny's vehicle.

Sonny put his Glock back in the holster he wore on the back of his belt, always wearing some sort of a jacket to cover it. "What's this guy up to?" he wondered out loud, sounding frustrated and scanning all around the area.

"Not sure," Dillon said, holstering his Ruger, "but, let's go back and join the girls for now."

"Yeah, let's not ruin their night. And I'm sure Vicki is wondering what's up."

They returned to the table, and had drinks waiting for them. "No luck?" Sonja asked.

"Nope. The Camaro's still there, but no one's home," Sonny said, shrugging his shoulders.

"Here's to Saturday night," Dillon said, raising his drink and smiling.

"To Saturday night!" the other three chimed in, raising their drink glasses. They clinked glasses with one another, then drank from them.

"Sonja explained to me about the black Camaro while you were gone," Vicki said. "No idea who the guy is?"

"None at all. I was hoping we could finally find out something when Dillon spotted him tonight. But, it'll wait. We're not going to let him ruin our evening."

"Our waiter will be back with menus pretty quick," Sonja told them.

Jax Café is one of the few remaining classic restaurants in the Twin Cities area. Opened in the late 1930s, the Kozlak family has preserved its rich tradition and promise of uncompromised service for more than eighty years. They specialize in serving the finest cuts of beef and fresh seafood flown in from all over the world. Jax is a true Nordeast Institution. And, without question, Sonny's favorite restaurant of all time.

Nearly finished with her lobster, Sonja excused herself to go to the ladies room. "I'll join you," Vicki said, wiping her mouth lightly with her napkin, and placing it next to her plate.

The two were gone for several minutes, then returned to the table rather hurriedly. "Sonny... Sonny," Sonja said, in a whisper that was almost a shout. "He's sitting at the bar."

"The guy from the black Camaro?"

"Yeah, the one who brought me the letter then got in the black Camaro, he's sitting at the bar. He stared at me when I came out of the ladies room. He's on the third stool."

Sonny and Dillon pushed back their chairs and jumped to their feet, hurrying toward the bar area. Both held their hand on their weapons, but did not draw them.

Sonny quickly scanned the bar, looking for the third stool. It was empty, with a half full drink sitting on the bar. "He's gone. Must've realized that Sonja recognized him."

"Check outside," Sonny said, hurrying toward the door. Dillon was close behind.

Reaching the sidewalk, they saw the Camaro doing a quick U-turn and heading north on University. "One day were going to meet this guy face-to-face," Sonny growled.

They both secured their weapons in their holsters and walked back to the waiting girls.

"Got away again," Dillon said to the women, sounding very frustrated.

"Yeah, but one of these times he's going to slip up and we'll introduce ourselves," Sonny said. "Meanwhile," he said smiling, trying to brighten the mood, "how about a good after dinner drink."

Chapter Twenty-Nine

"To live happily is an inward power of the soul."
Marcus Aurelius (121 – 180 AD)

Early Monday morning, Sonny's phone rang. He was just finishing his morning ritual of shaving, showering, and brushing his teeth. He grabbed the hand towel from the vanity, dried his hands and mouth, then reached for his phone. As he picked it up, he noticed the time display said 7:27, and the caller ID read Dan "Too Tall" Moretti. He smiled to himself. He liked Dan a lot.

Dan Moretti had carried the nickname "Too Tall" since he was a junior in high school. At that time he was three inches taller than anyone in the school, including all the adults. Today he stands 6'10", a towering figure. Dan is the owner and manager of Nicolette Bail Bonds in downtown Minneapolis.

Sonny touched a button on his phone to answer the call. "Good morning Dan," he said brightly.

"Good morning Sonny, it's been a while. Things are good with you, I hope."

"They are… very good! What can I do for you on this wonderful Monday morning?"

"Well, you know the routine Sonny. I've got one that I let out way too much line on. Like always, hoping he might get picked up by a local for speeding, or whatever, and save me a bundle. Now I've only got a month and a half left to bring him in before I'm on the hook for two hundred thousand. Any chance you can help me in the next week?"

"You're in luck, Dan. Our schedule is clear this week and next week. Are you in your office already this morning?"

"No, I'll be in there about eight-thirty if you wanna come over and get a copy of our file."

"How about I darken your door at nine o'clock. What kind of character is this skip?"

"Well, he's up on a couple of different drug charges, but he's only 5'8" and 150 pounds. I'm guessing you could handle him with one hand behind your back."

"Okay," Sonny said, chuckling. "See you at nine."

"Thanks Sonny, I really appreciate it. See you in a little while."

Sonny hung up his phone and slid it into his pocket. He picked up a comb and ran it through his hair a couple of times, then tossed the comb back on the vanity as he turned and headed for the kitchen.

He made himself a quick breakfast of scrambled eggs, toast, and orange juice. At eight-forty he was backing out of his driveway and was off to visit Too Tall and the offices of Nicolette Bail Bonds.

He parked in the ramp across the street and walked in the front door, saying, "Good morning, Alexa, great to see you again." Alexa was an attractive, slim, and very tall woman, nearly 6' 4" tall. She was Too Tall's daughter. The oldest of his three daughters.

"Good morning, Sonny, great to see you, too. My dad said you were coming in this morning, so just go on back." She reached for the intercom button to let her dad know.

"Thanks, Alexa," Sonny said, and started toward Dan's office. "Are you still seeing that guy... Jim was it?" he said, pausing as he passed her desk.

She just smiled and nodded her head.

"Good for you! He seems like a decent guy," Sonny said, continuing toward Dan's office.

Dan was standing in the doorway and reached out his hand as Sonny neared. "Good morning. Great to see you," he said. "It's been a couple months since you last visited our humble offices."

Sonny shook his hand, saying, "Yes, it's been at least two months. Things must be going pretty good for you in the bail bond world with very few skips."

"Yes," Dan said, knocking on the wood frame around his office doorway. "Come on in." He sat in an easy chair next to Sonny, and reached for a file on his desk. Handing the file to Sonny, he said, "I'll let you decide how you'll go about locating this guy, but, from everything I know, all his connections are in the Camden area of North Minneapolis."

"Good to know. I'll start digging into the file later this morning with Dillon. We've been getting busier lately, so I've started bringing him in on all of our cases – not just the ones that pose a serious physical threat. I'll keep you informed every day or two on our progress, and hopefully have the guy checked into the Hennepin County Jail in the next two weeks for you."

"That'll be a lifesaver, as usual," Dan said.

"Still playing basketball over at the U of M with your crew of alumni?" Sonny asked.

"Yeah, but I've cut back to just once a week. By the time you shower, get dressed, and have some lunch, half of the day is shot. So, I'm only getting a good workout once a week now."

"I'd say, for a man who's just on the south side of forty," Sonny said, "that's not too bad. The way you guys play, I'd say it's probably a mighty good workout."

"Yeah, you're right," Too Tall said, smiling and standing from his chair.

Sonny stood and looked up at Dan, saying, "I'll call you in the next day or so, when we've figured out how we're going at this."

"Thanks, Sonny. Whenever you take a case for us, I know I don't have to worry about it any longer."

Chapter Thirty

"He who lives in harmony with himself
lives in harmony with the universe.
Marcus Aurelius (121 – 180 AD)

Leaving Too Tall's office, and the downtown area, Sonny called Dillon on the phone. "I just got a new file from Too Tall. Any chance you can meet me at my place about eleven this morning?"

"Yeah. I was just gonna call you and see what's on the docket for today. How about we go to Shaws for lunch after we go over that file? I'm hungry for a good Sunburger."

"Sounds good. See you at eleven... or about ten minutes to." Sonny could hear Dillon chuckling, as he lowered his phone and clicked off the call.

At ten minutes to eleven, as expected, Dillon rang Sonny's doorbell and walked in. "Mornin'," Sonny said, as Dillon walked over and pulled out a chair across from him.

"Mornin' Big Guy. What's the deal with this new skip?" he asked, as he settled onto the chair.

"The skip, Damon Boudrais, is up on a fourth degree drug charge, which I think carries up to fifteen years. And with his rap sheet, I'm sure he'd be lookin' at ten to fifteen. Too Tall said that most of his contacts were in the Camden area. The stuff on his rap sheet shows the same. The question is, with this hanging over his head, is he still in the area?"

Sonny had made a full copy of the file for Dillon. He slid it across the table, saying, "Here's your copy. From now on you get a full copy of our file so you can look at it at home... or wherever. Maybe find something in there we hadn't noticed before."

"Not a bad idea. Never liked the paperwork, but I guess it'll be helpful to be able to review things."

"So far, I haven't seen any contacts or places to start looking for this guy," Sonny said, sounding frustrated.

For the next half hour, they sat in silence reading the file. Finally, Sonny said, "Do you remember the small-time dealer from the Camden area? I think we picked him up on a ten thousand dollar bond – stumbled across him while we were tracing a bigger fish for Saul. The small-timer ended up serving forty days, if I remember right. And I think he went by the nickname "The Fin.""

"Yeah, I remember him," Dillon said. "His dad was a big Finlander... remember that guy? A tough old bird, that didn't like his son messin' in the drug world."

"That's the one! Why don't we go look him up? See if he knows this guy Charles Boudrais."

"Sounds like as good a place to start as any," Dillon said. "Now, why don't we first head for Shaws and a delicious Sunburger."

Chapter Thirty-One

"To live happily is an inward power of the soul."
Marcus Aurelius (121 – 180 AD)

After a good lunch and a chat with Mike Shaw, the owner, they drove across the Lowery Bridge into the Camden area, and headed for T-Willie's. It had been nearly a year and a half, so they weren't sure if 'The Fin' still hung around there. But it had been the bar of choice for both he and his dad, and they hoped one or both still drank there.

They walked in the front door and saw four customers scattered along the bar. They didn't recognize any of them as The Fin, or his dad, so they walked to the corner of the bar and two empty stools. The bartender walked over, saying, "What can I get you gentlemen?"

"Have you got Grain Belt in a bottle?" Sonny asked.

"Sure do. Want one of those?"

"Yeah. And a glass, please."

As the bartender looked toward Dillon, he said, "I'll have the same."

"Comin' right up," the bartender said, as he moved down the row of shining metal tops on the beer coolers.

Returning with two bottles of Grain Belt and two empty glasses, he slid them in front of Sonny and Dillon.

As he did that, Sonny asked, "Say do you know if The Fin or his dad still come in here?"

"Yeah, Niko, his dad, comes in here most days around one-thirty for a couple of beers... after his wife fixes him lunch.

"His kid, The Fin," the bartender said, raising his hands to do air quotes, while seeming to be unimpressed with the kid, "I see maybe a couple times a week. Why you asking?"

"Oh, I just wanted to ask the kid about a friend of his," Sonny said. "He gave me his number once before, but I lost it. And the kid must have a new phone number. I haven't talked to him for almost a year and the number I have for him isn't working."

"We'll just have to stop by in the early afternoon and catch Niko sometime," Dillon said. "It'd be fun to see him and talk to him again."

"What's your name's?" the bartender asked, reaching for a pencil on the cash register. "I can let them know you stopped in and are looking for them."

"No," Sonny said, slowly, "you don't have to bother with that. Like Dillon said, we'll just stop in one afternoon and catch up with Niko."

"Okay," the bartender said, shrugging and setting the pencil back on the cash register. "Like I mentioned, you can catch him in here most days around one thirty."

Sonny thanked the bartender and asked him for a bag of pretzels, pointing to the rack on the back wall of the bar.

"No need," the bartender said, reaching for a small bowl on the shelf under the bar. He took the lid off a large plastic container of pretzels and poured some into the bowl. "It's happy hour from three to six. Free pretzels!"

"Well thanks," Sonny said and smiled.

The two sat munching pretzels and sipping Grain Belt beer, and talking in low voices about returning the next afternoon – and as many afternoons as needed – to catch up with Niko and see what he would tell them about his kid.

The next day, Sonny and Dillon sat on the same barstools at T-Willie's. A few minutes past one-thirty, Niko walked in. The bartender, whose name is Richard, called out, "Hey, Niko, come on down here."

"What's up, Richard?" Niko asked as he neared

Richard waved a finger at Sonny and Dillon, saying, "These two gentlemen wanted to speak with you."

"Hello Niko," Dillon said, sitting closest to him. "Don't know if you remember us, we did some businesses with your son last year."

Sonny stood from his barstool and reached around Dillon, saying, "Hi Niko. I'm Sonny."

"Sonny," Niko said, sounding a little surprised. "You I remember. That was some kind of business with my son."

"Yeah... well... he was trying to skip out on his bail. If you think back, you weren't too pleased with him about it at that time either."

"Got that right," Niko said, sternly. "I probably gave him more grief than the cops did. *AND*, after serving forty days and thinking about what it might be like to serve hard time, he decided to take my advice and stay away from the drugs. He's been clean for a year now. What do you want with him?"

"Grab the stool," Sonny said, pointing to the one next to him. "Let us buy you a beer."

Chapter Thirty-Two

"Give yourself a special gift: the present moment."
Marcus Aurelius (121 – 180 AD)

Working on their second round of beers, Sonny explained to Niko that they were hoping his son might know something about a skip they were tracing. "The guy's name is Charlie 'Tom-Tom' Boudrais. He's real heavy into the drug business and we're trying to figure out if he's still working the Camden area. We were just hoping your son might know the guy, and know something about where he's at or what he's up to. There's five hundred dollars in it for your son, for information that leads us to Tom-Tom. And another thousand if it helps bring him in."

Niko sat up straighter on his barstool, saying, "That's not chicken feed. I hope Danny knows something about this Tom-Tom character. He's stopping over to the house about five-thirty this evening and having supper with us. You're welcome to come over and talk to him."

"I think we'll take you up on that invitation, Niko," Sonny said. "But I think it would be better if you didn't say anything to Danny before we get there. It might panic him."

"Okay, I'll go along with that. Why don't you come about six-fifteen when we're finishing up with dinner."

"We'll see you at six-fifteen then," Sonny said. "Just so you know, Danny's name will never be mentioned, not even to the police. So he won't have to worry about anything coming back at him."

That evening, they rang the doorbell at Niko's home. Niko, expecting them, went to the door and welcomed Sonny and Dillon into their home. "Come in gentlemen, please. Danny, I think you know these men. They're here because they need your help."

Danny was a little surprised by the situation. His mom was calm and pleasant, because Niko had explained the reason for their visit.

"My help?" Danny said, sounding indignant and turning back to finish his supper.

"Daniel, these men are guests in our home and you'll treat them with respect," Niko said, sternly. "Besides, I think you should tell them thank you for helping you get clean."

"Please, no thanks are necessary from Danny, Mr. Heikkinen... Niko," Sonny said. "In similar circumstances, I might be a little angry, too."

"Danny, Loretta, come sit with us in the living room," Niko said, steering Sonny and Dillon toward the couches and easy chairs. "Can I get you anything to drink?"

Dillon held up a hand, indicating he didn't need one, and Sonny said, "Thank you, but were just fine."

"So, how is it that I can be of help to you?" Danny asked, dropping down in an easy chair.

"We've been hired to bring Charlie Boudrais in to the Hennepin County Jail," Sonny said. "I know you're familiar with the kind of work we do.

148

"Tom-Tom Boudrais is up on far worse charges then you were a year and a half ago. We're trying to find out where he's selling these days. There's a five hundred dollar reward if you have information on where he's at. And another thousand dollars if we collar him and bring him in to the Hennepin County authorities."

"That's serious money, son," Niko said.

"Do you know anything about this Boudrais guy?" Loretta, his mom, asked.

"If I do," Danny said slowly, "How do I keep from being buried in the woods somewhere, or floating down the bottom of the Mississippi?"

"I told your Dad earlier," Sonny said, "and I'll guarantee it to you, that no one will ever hear your name. Not even the police."

"Sure thing," Danny said, scoffing. "How do I know you can guarantee it at all?"

"Because I'm giving you my word," Sonny said, looking at him more seriously than Danny had ever seen before. "And my word is more important than just about anything for me. This is just us talking in this room, no one else will ever hear about it from me or Dillon. So, if you never say anything to anyone, no one knows but us."

Danny paused, staring down at his hands and considering it. "Okay," he finally said, "here's the deal. I've got info, but it's seven-fifty up front and twelve-fifty more if you bring him in. "

"Quite the negotiator you've raised," Sonny said, smiling at Loretta. "You've got a deal. What do you know about Tom-Tom Boudrais?"

"It's been a few months since I've seen him," Danny said, "but I know he was working St. Cloud hard to expand his business. So he spends about a third of his time in the Camden area and two thirds in St. Cloud."

"Does he live in the Camden area?" Dillon asked.

"Yeah, I don't know the house number, but he lives in the top floor of a huge house on Webber Parkway. He and his girlfriend have been there for at least two years now."

"How about St. Cloud?" Sonny asked. "Any idea where he hangs out there?"

"I heard that he drinks at the Red Dog Saloon, off Highway 23."

"How about Camden, any particular bar he hangs out at?" Dillon asked.

"No, he hits all the bars in the area. Makes contact with his people and moves on."

Chapter Thirty-Three

"The art of living is more like wrestling than dancing."
Marcus Aurelius (121 – 180 AD)

Sonny paid Danny seven hundred and fifty dollars in cash and shook his hand. "Thanks, I hope we'll be back soon with another twelve-fifty for you." Then he and Dillon thanked Niko and Loretta and left their home.

"S-o-o-o," Dillon said slowly, as they walked down the sidewalk, "where do you wanna start with Tom-Tom?"

"Well, even though he might be spending lots of time in St. Cloud, according to Danny, let's try and find the place where he lives on Webber Parkway."

"Starting tomorrow afternoon?"

"How about we meet at my place... two o'clock."

At ten minutes before two, Dillon rang Sonny's doorbell and walked in. Sonny was at his desk, and shouted, "In here, Dillon. Come on in."

Dillon took a seat in one of the three easy chairs across from Sonny's desk. "What'cha thinkin'? How do you want to go after this Boudrais character?"

"Webber Parkway is only six blocks long, and there are two different access streets across from the homes that go into Webber Park. Let's take both vehicles, that way we can cover the whole area watching for him or his gal."

"That works for me. Didn't Danny say that Boudrais drives a dark blue Riviera with flashy wheels? Shouldn't be that tough to spot if he comes down the Parkway."

As they walked out the door, Sonny said, "Give me a radio check before we head out."

"Will do," Dillon said, walking toward his car.

Dillon followed Sonny to the Webber Parkway area, trailing by a couple minutes so they wouldn't be noticed pulling in at the same time. Sonny pulled in the far entrance near the Rec Center, and found a place to park his vehicle that faced the homes across Webber Parkway. Dillon pulled in the first entrance to the park area, and situated himself in the same fashion.

Sonny was settling in and scanning the homes with his binoculars. He keyed his radio, saying, "I've got a good view of things from here. How about you?"

Dillon lowered his binoculars and grabbed the radio from the passenger seat. "Yeah, I've got a good view of everything from Aldrich to Dupont. Although it's a little tricky to see what might be going on at the last two houses near Dupont."

"That's okay. I can see those two houses and their driveways pretty good. So, now, it's just watch and wait."

"Roger that," Dillon said. "Next check-in time will be five o'clock. Talk to you then." He put the radio back on the passenger seat, then reached in the back seat for his pack and brought it up to the front.

He dug in his pack and brought out a bottle of water and an apple, then got comfortable in the driver's seat. The next two hours went by slowly, quietly. Other than a brief radio check at the top of each hour, there was nothing happening. At seven o'clock, Sonny made their usual radio check, and asked, "See those kids on the bikes over near the pond? It's amazing the stuff they can do."

"Yeah, I've been trying hard not to get too distracted watching them. You ever do tricks like that on your bike when you were a kid?"

"R-i-i-g-h-t," Sonny said slowly. "We never even thought about tricks like that when we were kids. Riding no-handed all over town was as tricky as we got. Like you said, though, it's hard not getting distracted and miss something happening across the street."

"Stay focused. Talk to you in an hour."

It was nearing eight o'clock and Dillon was thinking of picking up his radio for their hourly check-in. Suddenly, he saw Sonny's Tahoe pull out onto Webber Parkway in a mighty big hurry. Before he could key his radio to ask what was up, he heard Sonny almost shouting at the radio.

"Stay here and keep watching Dillon," Sonny said, loudly. "I'm headed for Sonja's. The black Camaro is there."

"I'm going with you Sonny," Dillon said, urgently.

"Thanks, but she's called 9-1-1 and their only five minutes away. I'm headed down there just in case. I'll call and let you know what's up, as soon as I find out."

The drive from the Camden area to Sonja's home in Eagan would normally take about thirty-five minutes. Sonny was there in nineteen minutes. As he jumped from the Tahoe, two Eagan police officers stopped him, asking, "Excuse us sir, but who are you?"

"I'm Sonny... her fiancé. She's expecting me."

"Mr. Sawyer?" one of the officers asked.

"Yes, that's me." Sonny grabbed his wallet and showed them his ID.

"Go ahead. Miss Wilkinson is in the kitchen with two of our detectives."

Chapter Thirty-Four

"Time. How brief and fleeting our allotment of it."
Marcus Aurelius (121 – 180 AD)

Sonja stood and hugged Sonny when he walked in the kitchen. They hugged for a long moment, then Sonny looked into her eyes, asking, "You okay, Babe?"

"Yeah, Sonny, I'm fine. I didn't want to panic you and make you come all the way down here."

"You know better than to worry about that," he said, then looked at the two detectives sitting at the kitchen table. "Are you gentlemen done with Sonja? If not, I'll stay out of the way until you finish your questioning."

"Just a couple more items," one of the detectives said. "Then we'll be on our way."

Sonny smiled at her and tilted his head toward the detectives. Then he went in the living room and sat on the couch. In less than ten minutes, the detectives were done and saying their goodbyes. Sonny walked back in the kitchen, waved to the detectives as they left, and gave Sonja another big hug. "Let's sit down and you tell me all about it. Every little detail. Don't leave out a single thing.

"And I could use a beer," he added. "I'll grab the beers, you grab the mugs." When they sat at the table, he said, "I better call Dillon first and let him know what's going on. We started that stakeout on Webber Parkway, and I asked him to keep watch while I come here."

Sonny pulled his phone from his pocket, punched in Dillon's number and, as he heard it start to ring, said, "I'm sure he's wondering what's up... and if you're okay."

Dillon answered and Sonny explained that everything was okay with Sonja. "I'm just getting a chance to sit down with her now and get the details of what happened. I'll update you later. How's things in Camden?"

"Still quiet," Dillon answered. "No sign of Boudrais. I'm probably going to pack it in by one-thirty if nothing changes. There's no lights on in any of the upper levels... where Boudrais is supposed to be living."

"Sounds good. Give me a call when you're ready to pack it in."

He hung up his phone, slid it on the table, then took a long drink of beer. "Okay! Details... gimme all the details."

"Well, I was on the couch talking to my mom on the phone, when I heard the doorbell ring and someone knocking loudly. Luckily, as I walked toward the door, I caught a glimpse of the black Camaro through the kitchen window. I paused, my hand on the door, and decided not to open it. *And* – you'll be so proud of me – I didn't look through the peep hole. It was hard, but I didn't look."

During one of his "lectures" (Sonny didn't consider them lectures, but on occasion Sonja did) about keeping herself safe, he stressed, "Never look out a peep hole. If someone is serious about hurting or killing you, they can just wait until they see the little glass go dark and shoot you right through the eye."

"So, I moved to a place where I couldn't be seen from outside and called 9-1-1. Then I called you. When I hung up from you, I stood there still as I could, listening hard for anything outside. Then I heard the rumble of the Camaro's engine starting and hurried to look out the window. I only caught a glimpse of it pulling away. That's it!" she said, holding up her hands. "That's all there is."

Sonny sat staring at his beer, slowly turning the glass on the table as he stared. "What'cha thinkin'?" Sonja asked, smiling softly at him.

"I am wondering if it's you he's after... and not me," he said, and looked up at her.

"Well, I've thought about that myself. But, for the life of me, I can't figure out *any* reason someone might be coming after me."

"No, you're right, it makes no sense. Which is part of the problem, some things happen that don't seem to make any sense at all."

Sonja got up from her chair and walked around behind Sonny. She leaned over, hugged him around his neck, and kissed him on the cheek. "Better call Dillon and update him. He's probably sitting there worried. Tell him you're staying here with me tonight, to make sure everything is okay and make sure I'm safe."

Sonny looked up and smiled at her, as he reached for his phone. "It's nice when we're thinking on the same wavelength," he said, then turned his attention to dialing Dillon's phone number.

Sonny finished his call to Dillon and slid the phone back on the table. Then he grabbed his glass of beer and finished what was left. He was about to ask for one more, but Sonja was already headed for the refrigerator.

"Everything okay with Dillon?" she asked, handing him another beer.

"Yeah, all is quiet. We're gonna meet at my place tomorrow afternoon at two o'clock, and do the stakeout routine again on Webber Parkway."

Chapter Thirty-Five

"Be indifferent to what makes no difference."
Marcus Aurelius (121 – 180 AD)

Sonja and Sonny moved into her living room and sat together on the couch. "After this beer, I think I'll switch to a little Glenfiddich over an ice cube," Sonny said.

"Good idea. Think I'll switch to a glass of wine. There should be some Pinot Noir left in the fridge."

"S-o-o-o," Sonny said slowly, "the question is... Why would the guy be after you?"

"I've given it a lot of thought and I always come up with a great big nothing."

"You haven't moved the family of a gangster lately?"

"No, not that I know of anyway," she said, shrugging.

"No drug lords or anyone that would be deep in the swill and the muck... dealing on the dark side?"

"Jesus no, Sonny. You spend most of your time chasing bad guys, and I hope it's not affecting your outlook on life and people."

"No, it's not Babe. This guy has just managed to get under my skin. I usually don't let that happen, but this guy... I just want to get my hands on this guy. Harassing you the way he has, I just want to get him in my grip."

"Well, so far," Sonja said, trying her best to sound optimistic, "he's only been a nuisance."

Sonny finished his beer and stood from the couch. "One Glenfiddich and one Pinot Noir coming right up."

"Sounds good. I'll put on some music."

He returned and walked over to where Sonja was putting Taj Mahal CDs on her player. Then they got comfortable on the living room floor and listened to the blues as they *should* be played. They laid there on the floor, couch pillows tucked under their heads, until Taj Mahal sang them both to sleep. After a while, Sonja nudged Sonny. "Let's go into bed. I've got an early meeting in Eden Prairie."

Sonny groaned and worked his way to his feet. "Eden Prairie... on Bear Path Golf Course I suppose."

"Well yes, in fact, it is. He's an attorney, a partner with the Johnson Day Law Firm. They're moving him to Atlanta to be the managing partner of that office. They've got a house full of antiques, and some fragile glass stuff. Fortunately, some people told him we were the best specialty movers."

"Sounds like a nice job. Freeways all the way to Atlanta aren't there?"

"Yup, it'll be a nice one. And a quick one. We have to start packing them up in two days and be in Atlanta in six."

"Wow," Sonny said, as they headed down the hallway toward the bedroom. "You guys must have quite the system for packing and securing everything. How many will you have working with you over there?"

"Five packing and me logging the inventory of each piece... and the condition each one. If we need any special crates, we've got three people back in the shop to build them and get them out to us."

At ten minutes before two the next afternoon, Dillon rang Sonny's doorbell and walked in. Sonny was at the kitchen table having a late lunch, and asked, "Hungry?"

"No, I had lunch already," Dillon said, pulling out a chair across from Sonny. "But thanks anyway."

They sat talking about Webber Parkway and their hopes of finding Boudrais, when Sonny's phone rang. He glanced at the screen and saw it was Dan "Too Tall" Moretti. Reaching for the phone, he told Dillon, "It's Too Tall."

He answered the phone, saying, "Hello Dan. How's things?" Dillon thought Sonny's face was turning a little pale as he listened to Too Tall for a bit.

"You're kidding me!" Sonny finally said, leaning back in his chair and looking at Dillon. He listened again, for what seemed like a long time without saying anything. He was occasionally looking at Dillon and slowly shaking his head, back and forth.

"They used duct tape and strapped his wrists to the wheel?" Sonny asked. Then he covered the phone with his hand, and quickly whispered to Dillon, "Boudrais is dead!"

"I know," Sonny said. "That's one I've never heard before. Never even thought of before. Sounds like something out of an old gangster movie." He was slowly shaking his head again as he listened.

"Don't worry about that, Dan. Nothing any of us could have done. Just one of those weird ones we can tell our grandchildren about."

"Okay Dan. Thanks for calling and letting us know." Sonny ended the call and slid the phone on the table.

He shook his head again, as though he couldn't believe what he'd just heard. "Somebody drugged Boudrais, then pulled his car onto the railroad tracks just outside of Cable – a little town southeast of St. Cloud. Then they duct taped his wrists to the steering wheel... in case he came to, I suppose.

"A freight train hit the car, still doing about fifty miles an hour. Sounds like everything was completely demolished, including Boudrais. They're speculating that it was drug rivals that didn't like him moving in on their territory."

Dillon sat staring at Sonny for a long moment. "That's a new one. I guess were all done with the Boudrais case."

"Yeah, Too Tall wanted to offer something for our time, but I told him no. It's all a part of doing business."

Chapter Thirty-Six

"Glory is an empty, changeable thing; as fickle as the weather."
Marcus Aurelius (121 – 180 AD)

Since they didn't have the stakeout to work on, Dillon thought he'd use the time to make a list of bail bondsman in the greater Twin Cities area that they hadn't done work for, and spend time calling on each of them.

The contract Dillon had with Sonny paid him forty percent of their commissions. That covered all of the bail bondsman that Sonny had brought in through his efforts. An addendum they'd just added to the contract, gave Dillon fifty-five percent of commissions from bondsmen that Dillon secured through his efforts. This offered great incentive for Dillon to go out, knock on doors, and try to sell their services to bail bondsmen they hadn't worked with in the past.

In a short while, Dillon had compiled a list of sixteen offices and began calling to schedule appointments with the person in charge of hiring Skip Tracers. By five o'clock that afternoon, Dillon had scheduled nine appointments.

"Wow," Sonny said. "That's impressive. Good work. Hopefully you can get us a couple new sources of business."

"We can only hope," Dillon said. "Call me if anything comes up, otherwise I'll be out knocking on doors and drumming up business."

"That works for me. I wanted some time to dig into this character with the black Camaro. So, unless somebody has an urgent skip they want brought in, we can be busy with our own stuff for the next few days.

At 5:15, Sonny was waiting for Sonja. He'd spoken with her briefly, and she said she'd be calling it a day and be home in a half hour. At 5:25 his phone rang and he hoped it wasn't her calling to say she had to work later.

He reached for his phone and saw it was the Minneapolis Police Department calling. He picked it up, touched the "Answer" button that was blinking, and said, "Hello, this is Sonny."

"Mr. Sawyer," the voice on the other end said, "this is Detective Helgeson of the Minneapolis Police Department. If I understand correctly, you are the person who asked the Eagan Department to issue a BOLO on a black Camaro."

"Yes, that's right Detective. Has something popped on it recently?"

"Yes, it was parked at an expired meter for almost seventy-two hours and then towed to the impound lot. An officer noticed it and remembered reading the BOLO. My partner and I checked it out about a half-hour ago, and it looks like it was thoroughly cleaned. Not a fingerprint to be found, other than the driver who hauled it in."

"Who is it registered to?" Sonny asked.

"The owner is a guy in Mankato, Minnesota, who reported it stolen a month ago."

"Interesting," Sonny said, then was silent for a long moment. "Sounds like a dead-end situation."

"Not completely. There was an eyewitness to the guy who broke in and stole the car. The witness worked with their police sketch artist, and the system came up with one match that really looks a lot like the sketch."

"Do you have an ID on the guy?" Sonny asked.

"Yes. His name is Sergei Petrov. He is a Russian, whose thought to have ties with the Kazakov family out of Fort Myers, Florida."

"Kazakov family..." Sonny said, haltingly. "Why does that name ring a bell?"

"You probably read about them a couple years ago. They had stolen two Van Gogh's and a Monet about eighteen years ago. They were terrifically clever thieves, but terrible businessmen."

"Why's that?"

"Well, they got away with stealing the paintings, only to find they couldn't sell them, even on the black market. No one in the art world would pay a nickel for stolen masterworks."

"So," Helgeson continued, "when they tried to peddle them again two years ago, they were caught."

"Yeah, I guess I do remember reading about that story," Sonny said. "What did this Petrov character have to do with the whole thing?"

"Well, the FBI's Art Crime Team was convinced that he was somehow in on it with the Kazakov family. They worked hard for months, but were never able to prove anything against him, so he walked."

"Okay. Now we just have to figure out what he wants with me or Sonja... or both of us."

"Not sure I can be of much help to you with that, but call if you have any questions."

The detective gave Sonny his direct number and said goodbye. Sonny laid the phone on his table and sat staring at it, wondering where to start with Sergei Petrov. His wondering was interrupted when he heard the garage door begin to open. When Sonja came through the door, he greeted her with, "Hey good lookin'," and gave her a big hug.

"Hey yourself," she said, and kissed him on the cheek.

"Want a beer or glass of wine with me?" he asked.

"Yeah, I'll have a Grain Belt, as soon as I change out of these clothes and throw on my sweats."

He opened a cold can of Grain Belt and set it on the table with a glass. Then he took a short, wide drink glass, dropped an ice cube in it, grabbed his bottle of Glenfiddich and set them on the table. He was just taking his first sip of the Scotch when she walked into the kitchen.

"I think you should be at the door to greet me whenever I come home," she said smiling. "It really does brighten things after a long day at the office." She circled the table to kiss him on the cheek again, then continued to her seat where the beer waited.

"I would love to be here every evening to greet you. But, you know my work. I'm only at home half the time."

"I know," she said, raising the glass of beer to toast him. "But... still...."

"Yes, I know," he said slowly. "And sometimes it's your turn to be here and greet me."

Chapter Thirty-Seven

"A thing is neither better nor worse for having been praised."
Marcus Aurelius (121 – 180 AD)

Sonny thought he would let Sonja drink some of her beer and unwind for a while, before bringing up his conversation with Detective Helgeson. They relaxed, enjoyed their drinks, and enjoyed each other, talking and laughing about little things... everyday things.

When she asked, "Anything new on the Camero?" he figured it was time to take things up a couple of notches on the "seriousness scale."

"Yes, I spoke with a Detective Helgeson from the Minneapolis Police Department. He called not more than a half hour ago."

"Are you in trouble?" she asked, sounding concerned.

"No... not at all. They had a hit on the BOLO for the black Camaro. It was abandoned... left at a parking meter long enough that they towed it to the impound lot."

"Really? Do they know who the owner is?"

"Yeah, but that doesn't help us. The owner is a guy in Mankato who reported it stolen a month ago. The good news is that there was an eyewitness who described the thief to a police sketch artist. They got a match with a guy who worked with some big-time art thieves out of Florida."

"What's that got to do with us?" she asked, a puzzled look on her face. Then she sat back and relaxed in her chair.

"Haven't a clue... *Yet*," he said.

He paused, giving it some thought, then tried to change the subject and lighten the mood a bit, asking, "Whad'aya feel like eating tonight? Pizza? Chinese? Some other kind of order out goodies? I don't feel like cookin' this evening, and I'm sure you don't either."

"You're right... I don't feel like cooking at all. Chinese... I vote for Chinese. I know you and Dillon have had some recently, but it's been a while since I've had any."

"Chinese it is then. You make the call for delivery from Leeann Chin. Just order two of whatever you like, 'cause you know I like it all."

It would be a half hour to forty minutes for delivery of their dinner, so Sonny decided to fire up his laptop and do a little research, see what he could find out about the Kazakov family. Hopefully find some clue how Sergei Petrov fits in to the whole situation.

Their dinner arrived, and Sonny continued to narrate his findings on the computer, giving Sonja the details of the art thefts by the Kazakovs. "It was thought that they had stolen a dozen valuable paintings between 1994 and 2009. The most valuable of which were two Vincent van Gogh paintings and one Claude Monet, taken from the Vincent van Gogh Museum in Amsterdam in 2008," Sonny said, pausing to dip his egg roll in the bowl of sweet-and-sour sauce.

He continued. "The Kazakov couple generally had a third person, and sometimes even a fourth depending on the difficulty of the job at hand, to help them in a number of ways." He paused again, eating more of the pork fried rice and lo mein. "Mmmm... this is all delicious!"

"Yes, it is," Sonja mumbled, her mouth half full of lo mein. She finished chewing and swallowing, then took a long drink of Grain Belt. Wiping her mouth with her napkin, she asked, "Anything in there about Petrov?"

"Nope. Not yet. There's a couple more pages to go, so hopefully his name comes up." He read on in silence for a while, eating more of his dinner. After a bit, he pointed at the computer's screen, saying, "Here it says that their helper on the 2005 heist was a native Russian that now lived in Miami. The three of them flew together to Amsterdam a month before the heist.

"We're getting closer," he said, eating more. "Since they're located in Fort Myers, Florida, it's not surprising that they connected up with a Russian from Miami."

He continued to read in silence, as before, finishing his dinner as he read. Nearing the end of the article, he said, "Says here that none of the paintings have been recovered. That goes back to what Detective Helgeson said about art thieves."

"What did he say?" Sonja asked.

"That they were extremely talented thieves, but terrible businessmen."

"Why does he think that?"

"Made sense... after he explained it. No serious collector would buy a valuable piece of art that was known to have been stolen. You could never tell anyone about it or display it. It would be a mighty rare bird that would pay big money for a stolen painting, only to have it in his private collection – never to be spoken of or shown to anyone."

Sonja finished her beer, wiped her mouth with her napkin again and laid it next to her empty plate. "It does make sense when you think about it that way."

"Wow!" Sonny said, reading further. "Only ten to fifteen percent of all valuable art that's stolen is ever recovered."

"So, where does it disappear to?"

Sonny slowly shook his head, and gave a low chuckle. "Again... I haven't a clue."

Chapter Thirty-Eight

"The only wealth you will keep forever is what you have given away."
Marcus Aurelius (121 – 180 AD)

Sonja's stay at Sonny's home had turned from one week into several, and Sonny was enjoying it. He liked having her around, and liked not worrying about her being alone in Eagan with this Petrov character roaming around.

Sonja had spoken with several of her neighbors, asking them to keep an eye out for anyone lingering around the neighborhood. The next evening, she received a call from Catherine, a very nice retired woman who lived directly across the street from Sonja's home.

"Hi Sonja," Catherine said, "you wanted to know if anyone was lingering around the neighborhood. Well, yesterday, there was a black SUV – my husband thought it looked like a Lincoln MKX – anyway, the guy was parked on our street for a couple hours. Then today, he was there again. This time, after an hour or so, he walked over to your mailbox, looked through your mail and put back in the box. Then he got in the SUV and left. Should I call the police?"

"No," Sonja said, "you don't have to call the police if he's gone. But thanks so much for keeping an eye out. Let me know if that SUV shows up again."

"I sure will," Catherine said.

After saying goodbye and hanging up her phone, Sonja told Sonny, "Sounds like our friend Petrov has a black SUV — maybe a Lincoln MKX — since abandoning the Camaro. Catherine saw it there yesterday and again today."

"That's good. At least we have *something* to work with on the guy. I think I'll spend some time the next few days doing a stake-out from inside your home. See if I can get a chance to meet him face-to-face."

The next morning at 5:30 AM, Sonny headed for Eagan. He knew he could avoid rush-hour traffic at that time, and wanted to get there before Petrov might be in the area. Arriving at Sonja's, he drove around the block several times checking to see if there was a black SUV. Then he pulled into Sonja's garage, closed the door and slipped into the house. He sat in the dark of the early morning, scanning the street for the SUV.

The morning passed slowly and at quarter to twelve Sonny fixed himself a "Dagwood" sandwich, with a couple of different lunch meats and cheese and onion and mustard. He ate it with potato chips and pickles and a tall glass of Pepsi. He shifted his position to where he was hidden from sight by the island counter in the kitchen, but still could see the street through a couple of different windows.

A half hour later, he saw the postman stop and put some mail in Sonja's powder-blue colored mailbox. About an hour later, Sonny noticed a black SUV pull up and park in the shade of the trees about four houses down from Sonja's. The driver turned off the engine, glanced around the neighborhood, then settled back in his seat as though planning to be there a while.

Sonny finished his sandwich, then quickly finished his glass of Pepsi. Glancing back at the SUV, he saw there was no one in it. Checking a second time, with binoculars, he concluded the SUV was indeed empty. Where had the guy gone so quickly?

Finally, he saw a shadow coming out from behind the garage. *Was it him? Was it Petrov?* The guy was slowly moving down the sidewalk, checking all of the neighboring homes. *To see if anyone had noticed him,* Sonny thought.

He was walking toward Sonja's mailbox. *Are you seriously gonna rifle through her mail again today?* he wondered. Then a small grin creased his lips. His foolishness was giving Sonny opportunity to sneak around the garage and get between him and his SUV. He hurried to the patio door, slid it open enough to sneak out, closed it quietly, then hurried around the garage. Petrov didn't see him, as he emerged from the other side of the garage.

Sonny stepped out onto the sidewalk and waited for Petrov to turn and head for the SUV. Finally closing the lid on Sonja's mailbox, then glancing around the neighborhood once more, Petrov turned to head back to his SUV – the stolen Lincoln MKX – and, for an instant, didn't notice Sonny blocking his way.

In the next moments, Petrov took one step, saw Sonny standing in his way, hesitated as though not sure what he would do, then bolted across the street hoping to get to the SUV before Sonny could run him down.

Sonny wasn't sure if Petrov was packing heat but held his hand on his Glock, which discouraged Petrov from drawing the Smith & Wesson he carried.

Sonny ran Petrov down, tackled him on the far side of the street, and the two wrestled in the neighbor's yard for a few seconds. Then Petrov struggled to his knees and threw the first punch. It was a roundhouse right and Sonny quickly turned his head and ducked, the blow glancing off the side of his forehead.

Sonny grabbed a fistful of Petrov's shirt, yanked him hard and head butted him – the top of his forehead hitting Petrov squarely on the bridge of his nose, breaking bone.

With the loud, scary sound of crunching bone, and blood gushing from his nose, Petrov held up his hands, saying, "Bol'she ne nado" – "No More. No More."

Sonny pulled his Glock and waved it toward a nearby tree. "On your feet... hands against that tree." As Petrov slowly stood and leaned against the tree, Sonny kicked the inside of his feet and Petrov spread his feet farther apart.

Sonny took the Smith & Wesson from Petrov's holster and slid it in the back of his own jeans. Then he frisked him for anything else he might be carrying. He found nothing, not even a wallet or any identification. Then he stepped back, saying, "Walk over to Miss Wilkinson's garage."

Petrov pushed away from the tree, one hand holding his bleeding nose. Muffled, he asked, "You got handkerchief or someting to stop bleeding?"

"You cooperate," Sonny said, "and I'll get you something to stop the bleeding. You don't cooperate and I'll bust it again."

He cooperated, and Sonny led him to the side door of the garage. They stepped in and he pushed the button for the garage door opener. As the door rolled up, Sonny grabbed a handful of paper towels from Sonja's workbench, then grabbed a bottle of water from his vehicle and handed them to Petrov.

"Blagodaryu vas" – "Thank you," Petrov said, wetting some of the paper towels and holding them tight to his nose.

When the bleeding seemed to be under control, Sonny put Petrov in handcuffs and led him into the back seat of his Tahoe, where he chained the cuffs to the D-ring bolted to the back seat floor. As Sonny slowly backed out of the garage and closed its door, Petrov asked with his thick Russian brogue, "Vere ve go?"

"Well, we're going to go visit the Hennepin County Sheriff's office in Minneapolis and see if you are willing to explain why you've been following me on a couple different occasions, and why you've been stalking Sonja Wilkinson at her home."

"I tell you notting."

"Ve haf vays to make you talk," Sonny said, with a poor imitation of a Russian brogue... and a grin.

"Vat you t'ink, you James Bond in da movie "From Russia with Love" or someting?"

"No," he said slowly, "but our police aren't like Inspector Clouseau in the Pink Panther either. They will find out what we need to know. And you can be sure that if they don't, I will be waiting for you when they release you and bust more than your nose." Sonny was quiet for the next fifteen minutes, letting Petrov think about it.

Sonny glanced in the mirror and thought Petrov looked a little nervous as he stared out the side window. "Well, got anything to tell me before we get to Hennepin County? We'll be there in ten minutes."

"No. I haf not'ing to say to you... or your Hennepin County people."

"Okay. Have it your way," Sonny said.

He exited 35W on 5th Avenue to downtown Minneapolis, then on to the Hennepin County jail. During Petrov's silence on the way downtown, Sonny had called ahead to let the Hennepin County people know he was bringing in Petrov and pressing charges. He parked near 4th Avenue and 5th Street, unchained Petrov from the D-ring and started to walk him toward the jail.

As they neared the entrance to the county jail, Petrov seemed to stumble. When Sonny tried to catch him and keep him from falling, Petrov planted his foot and swung his handcuffed arms hard towards Sonny's midsection. Sonny, always ready for a perp to try something like this quickly raised his knee and the back of Petrov's wrist hit solidly on the knee.

Sonny heard a loud, "Ahhhhhh," from Petrov and jerked him hard by the back of his shirt.

"Wanna try that again?" he growled, staring Petrov in the eyes.

Chapter Thirty-Nine

"Each day provides its own gifts."
Marcus Aurelius (121 – 180 AD)

An hour and a half later, Sonny left the Hennepin County jail and headed for home. He was hungry and anxious to see Sonja, and to give her the update on Petrov.

Waiting at a stop light, he checked his phone messages knowing that he had let at least one call go through. The call was from Frank Hahn, owner of the Northside Bail Bonds, and it sounded urgent. He pressed the telephone icon to return the call, and then the speaker symbol to lay the phone down and speak hands-free.

He heard Frank answer the call, and said, "Hey Frank, this is Sonny. How've you been?"

After some catching up chit-chat, Frank asked, "What's your schedule like for the next week?"

"Pretty good. What'cha got?"

"We've got a jumper that's got away twice on us. Not a real big deal, since it's only a thirty thousand dollar bond and we have a little time left, but still...."

"How about Dillon and I stop by your office at nine tomorrow morning? Talk about it and get a copy of your file."

"I don't think you'll need to hire Dillon," Frank said.

"We work together on everything now, so there's different charges for risky ones. You'll be getting our updated info."

"Okay! Sounds good," Frank said. "See you at nine o'clock tomorrow, then."

"See you then," Sonny said cheerfully, and clicked off the call. At home in his driveway, he called Dillon who said he'd be at Sonny's at eight o'clock the next morning.

He parked the Tahoe, went in the house and plopped down on his recliner to relax for just a minute. When Sonja came home an hour later, Sonny was sound asleep in the recliner. For the next half hour, she moved around quietly trying to let him sleep longer.

Finally, after changing clothes and pouring them each a drink, she walked over and softly kissed him on the cheek. He flinched, slightly startled, and then smiled as he looked up at Sonja.

"Hey gorgeous," he said, stretching for a moment. "Think I dozed off for a bit."

"Think you did... and I think you probably needed it. Ready for drink?"

"Love one," he said, standing up from the recliner.

They sat at the kitchen table and, as they sipped their drinks, Sonny asked, "How was your day?"

"Our day was great. All packed up and ready to roll toward Atlanta in the morning... a day ahead of schedule."

"Wow, ya gotta love that!"

"Yes, and our customer loves it too. Now," she said, leaning back in her chair, "tell me something good about our guy Sergei Petrov."

Sonny couldn't help but grin at her, then said, "He's locked up in the Hennepin County jail."

"Wow. What charges do they have him on?"

"Only mail theft for now. I got him on video taking the mail out of your mailbox. That was before I circled around the backyard and caught him. Mail theft is a federal offense and enough to hold him for a few days, then he'll appear before a judge for a bail hearing."

"How are we going to find out why he was stalking me in the first place?" Sonja asked, a puzzled look on her face.

"Not sure, yet, but Dillon and I will be working on that problem while you and your crew are headed for Atlanta."

Early the next morning, Sonja was riding shotgun as the Precision Movers' tractor-trailer headed toward Atlanta. They hoped to be at the customer's new home there by the following evening. The rest of her crew followed in the company's Suburban.

Meanwhile, Sonny and Dillon were headed for the offices of Northside Bail Bonds and their meeting with Frank Hahn. Frank gave them a copy of their file on the skip and explained that the guy was up on his third DUI and didn't present any kind of physical risk for Sonny and Dillon.

"Why the guy thought he could run from this third DUI… I'll never know. But he has… twice now. First time we caught him at his sister's home. Don't know where he might be headed this go-round."

"We'll find him for you and deliver him to the Hennepin County jail," Sonny said. "Hopefully within the next week."

"That would be great," Frank said. "I'm never concerned when you're on the job."

"That's good to know," Sonny said, reaching out to shake his hand. "That's always good to hear."

Back at Sonny's home, the two began analyzing Earl Roberts' file for any clue where to start searching. As they dissected each item in the file, Sonny said, "Earl lives in Blaine and is manager of Carlisle's Marketplace in Isanti. A third DUI might be heavily frowned on by the owners, and might even interfere with his ability to drive to and from work. Maybe he is showing up for work every day, trying to keep anyone from knowing."

"Let's pay the store a visit after lunch," Dillon said. Maybe go in one of the back delivery doors."

Sonny held up the photo of Earl Roberts saying, "This is the guy we'll be looking for. And a black, 2016 Chevy pickup with a flat hardcover on the box is the vehicle we'll be looking for."

After a quick lunch at Shaw's, they drove north on Highway 65 about thirty miles to Isanti. At the intersection with County Road 5, they swung around Carlisle's store to the delivery dock. They saw the black Chevy pickup parked next to the walk-in service door. The sign in front of the pickup read, "Reserved for Manager."

"That's gotta be his," Dillon said. "This is going to be way too easy."

"We can only hope," Sonny said, pulling the Tahoe directly behind the pickup and parking it close. "Don't want him driving away on us." He opened his door and slid from the Tahoe. Dillon did the same.

They quickly took the stairway to the loading dock and walked in the service door. Sonny led as they stepped in and scanned the area. Just then an employee stepped out of the walk-in cooler and closed its door. He looked at the two men, asking, "Can I help you gentlemen?"

"We have an appointment," Sonny said glancing at his watch, "with Earl, your manager. We're few minutes early, but could you see if he's available?"

"Sure thing," the young man said. "I think he's over in the meat department right now. I'll run and check for you."

"Thank you. That would be great," Sonny said. "We'll wait right here."

When the young man hurried toward the meat department, Sonny said, "I'm going to follow him. You wait here and cover the back. The guy might get crazy and bolt on us. Who knows? "

Sonny kept the young man in sight, trailing slowly behind. When the young man stopped in the meat department, he spoke to a gentleman wearing a shirt and tie. Soon there was a look of resignation on the older man's face. He turned and walked toward the back door looking for the guys with the appointment.

As he neared, Sonny reached out with a business card, saying, "I'm Harrison Sawyer. I'm here to bring you back to Hennepin County for your court hearing."

Earl stared at the card, and said, "I knew I didn't have an appointment."

"I can have my partner drive your pickup back to your home in Blaine if you'd like," Sonny offered.

"Can I ask a bigger favor?"

"You can ask," Sonny said with a shrug.

"My boss, the store owner, will be here in about twenty minutes. Can you let me explain to him before you take me back to Hennepin County? It's my only shot at saving my job."

Sonny looked into the man's eyes, and thought for a moment. "Okay. We'll wait. I've got the Tahoe that's parked right behind your pickup. You try to run again and it'll get real nasty."

"Thanks. I won't run. I'll be there as soon as I'm done with my boss."

Sonny explained to Dillon what he had agreed to, and said, "You wait in the Tahoe for Earl. I'm gonna circle around to the front and wait there, in case our friend tries anything stupid again."

Chapter Forty

"Conceal a flaw, and the world will imagine the worst."
Marcus Aurelius (121 – 180 AD)

They delivered Earl Roberts to the Hennepin County jail, then were bringing the paper work to Frank Hahn. Along the way Sonny said, "I was thinking..."

Dillon interrupted him, saying, "I was thinking the same thing. This was such a smooth and easy job, we should cut our fee."

"Yeah, our regular fee would be nearly six grand. Are you willing to go to four, since it was only one day and pretty easy besides? It would buy us a lot of goodwill with Frank."

"Yup. I can go along with that."

After delivering the paperwork and getting a check from Frank – who was more than grateful for their reduced fee – they headed for Sonny's home.

As they pulled in his driveway, Sonny said, "The only thing we've got to work on right now, is trying to get Petrov to tell us the reason he was stalking Sonja."

"I've been giving that some thought, too," Dillon said. "What if you didn't object to bail and, when they've released him, we grab him and put the squeeze on until he talks."

"Yeah, that may be our best bet on getting any info. It's not likely that the police will get the straight scoop from him. Particularly if he has any fear of the other Russians he works with... the art thieves.

That evening Sonja called to say their trip was going well and they hoped to be at the client's new home by four o'clock tomorrow afternoon. "If everything goes well with the unpacking, we should be back home in four days."

"Well, good luck then. I hope the unpacking goes smooth and nothing is damaged. Get yourself home by Saturday afternoon, so I can take you out to a nice dinner."

"I'll do my best. Hate to miss out on Saturday night with you. Love you, babe." She said goodbye and clicked off.

Sonny shut his phone off and smiled at it, thinking of Sonja and how much he'd missed her when she was on the road for more than a day or two.

Chapter Forty-One

"What is your mission? To be a good person."
Marcus Aurelius (121 – 180 AD)

At Petrov's bail hearing, the Hennepin County prosecutor offered no objection to bail, per the request of Sonny and Sonja. Bail was set at $25,000 and, after providing the required bond, Petrov was released and he climbed into a waiting green, Chevy crew cab pickup.

Outside the courthouse, Dillon waited to follow him in his pickup, one that Petrov would not recognize. To ensure that Petrov would not easily spot the tail, Dillon recruited his friend, Grant Daniels – a Sargent in the Army's military police who was home on leave – to tag team with him in following Petrov. They would trade off tailing him and keep in touch on their cell phone. They headed north on Third Avenue, then east on University Avenue toward St. Paul.

They tailed him to a home in the Frogtown area, where Dillon parked at the end of the block, several houses down from the front door Petrov entered. "Thanks, Grant, I owe you dinner tomorrow night. You choose the place." Dillon clicked off the call and laid his phone on the passenger seat, his eyes already scanning the house and yard of the home Petrov had entered.

After a few minutes, satisfied that everything was calm and quiet in the neighborhood, and the home where Petrov was, Dillon picked up his phone and called Sonny. "It's me. We followed him to a home at 753 Charles Ave. I'm parked at Avon and Charles, and the home is the fifth one on my left."

"Yup. I brought enough stuff for a good stakeout," he said, answering Sonny's question. "I'll keep in touch and call you right away if I need help."

"Alright, if you insist," Dillon said, again responding to Sonny. "Why don't you park at the other end of the block... at Charles and Grotto."

"Okay. Talk to you when you get here." Dillon clicked off his phone and dropped it on the passenger seat again. He grabbed a snack bar and bottle of water from his pack, got comfortable and was ready for a few good hours of surveillance.

After about forty minutes, Dillon's phone rang quietly. He glanced down and saw Sonny's name on the caller ID. He picked up the phone, clicked on the call and said, "Hey partner."

Sonny said, "You should see me coming around the corner and parking on Charles in a few seconds. Any activity since you got here?"

"Nope. All is quiet on the Eastern front. Is that you I see in a yellow pickup?"

"Yeah, it's my neighbors. He's got my Tahoe for the day. Since Petrov had tailed me a couple times, I figured he would recognize the Tahoe parked on his street."

"Good thinkin', partner."

"I suppose you don't know yet if Petrov is in there with only the one who picked him up, or with others?"

"I haven't seen anybody coming or going, but who knows how many were in there when he got home."

"Yeah, who knows what kind of a hornets nest we could be stepping into if we tried to take him out of there," Sonny said, sounding like he had resigned himself to the reality of a long stakeout.

It was a long and slow afternoon of watching the neighborhood and the home where Petrov was, with little or nothing happening. With everything this quiet they had no need to call except to check in at the top of each hour. As afternoon became evening and darkness overtook daylight, they still had seen no one coming or going at the house.

As lights came on in the homes, including Petrov's, Dillon called Sonny. "I'm going to do a little window peeping. See if I can figure out how many are in there with Petrov."

"Be careful out there, partner," Sonny said. "Put your phone in your pocket so I can call you if need be."

He clicked off the call, slid from the driver's seat, and put the phone in his back pocket. He double checked his Ruger and secured it back in its holster. Then he walked quietly to the side yard of the home where Petrov was. He began looking in windows, trying to see through gaps in draperies, above or below shades and curtains, anywhere to get a look inside. Finally, he saw Petrov and three others sitting at the kitchen table playing a card game that he didn't recognize. He had heard of a game called Durack, that someone said was a traditional Russian game.

None of the three playing with Petrov were as big as he, but they looked very capable nonetheless. He backed away from the window and moved to the other side of the neighbors bushes. Taking his phone from his back pocket, he called Sonny.

"Hey, looks like there's three others playing cards with Petrov in the kitchen right now. We could take them by surprise... no problem. Whadda'ya think?"

"I think you're right... but we don't know if there's anyone upstairs or downstairs that could turn the surprise back on us. I'd say it's safer to watch a little longer and see what happens. Agree?"

"Agree. I'm headed back to my vehicle. Later partner."

Chapter Forty-Two

*"When someone is properly grounded in life,
they have need to look outside themselves for approval."*
Marcus Aurelius (121 – 180 AD)

Sonny and Dillon spent another long hour watching. Finally, Petrov and the three card players came out the door, down the sidewalk, and slid into the green, crew cab pickup.

Dillon's phone rang and Sonny said, "They're headed my way. Why don't you take the first leg and we'll leapfrog 'em like you and Grant did earlier."

"Got it," Dillon answered, as he started his vehicle and put it in gear. "Stay on the phone so we can keep in touch all the way to wherever they're going."

"Roger that."

Dillon waited a moment for Petrov to turn right on Grotto, before turning on his headlights and following. As he passed the yellow pickup, he glanced and saw no one in it. Into his phone he said, "You laying down on the front seat or what? I didn't see anyone in there."

"Yeah, didn't want Petrov to see me. Guess it worked."

Dillon chuckled. "Looks like they're headed east on University. Talk to you soon." He turned left and fell in behind Petrov, trying to keep vehicles between them.

Soon he told Sonny, "Petrov's going left on Rice Street. You pick him up. I'll go straight ahead, take Jackson to Sycamore back to Rice, and fall in behind you."

189

"Okay. Got it."

Petrov came to a stop light and Sonny stopped with three vehicles between them. Petrov's next move was to take a left on Larpenteur Avenue. "We're heading west on Larpenteur," Sonny said, "Why don't you pass me and take over? I'll drop off for a bit."

"Just making the turn onto Larpenteur. I'll catch you in a half minute."

As Dillon passed him, Sonny turned right, went around the block, then turned right onto Larpenteur again, about a half-mile behind the Dillon. Soon, he heard Dillon say, "Now they're turning south on Lexington. Either they've changed their mind where they're going, or their taking the long way to see if they're being tailed. Your turn."

"I got 'em." Though it was a long two blocks ahead, Sonny could easily see the green pickup and saw Dillon turn off on Hoyt Avenue. They neared the Como Park area where Lexington Avenue wound its way through the golf course and park area. Sonny sped up to close the gap so he wouldn't lose Petrov while winding through the curves.

Finally, Lexington Avenue straightened out and Sonny could see Petrov's left turn signal blinking. "Looks like they're turning left on Front Avenue," he told Dillon.

"Maybe going to the Half Time Rec. If it looks like they're looking to park, we can turn south on Oxford and park a block away."

In less than a minute, Sonny was saying, "It's the Half Time Rec alright. They're driving slow looking for a place to park. I'm turning south on Oxford and will wait for you.

Sonny saw Dillon's pickup turn the corner and head toward him. He slid from the seat of the yellow pickup and waited for Dillon to pull over and park at the curb. He climbed in the passenger seat, saying, "That was a ten mile trip to go two miles. I think you were right. Either they couldn't make up their minds where they were going, or they were trying to spot a tail."

"Fortunately, I don't think they found the tail," Dillon said, clicking off his phone and laying it on the seat.

"What do you think about the odds... four against two?" Sonny asked, grinning at Dillon.

"Well, let them drink Russian vodka for a couple hours and I like the odds."

"That's what I was thinking, too. Why don't you go in first. Less likely they'll recognize you. Have your phone with you... just in case. I'll wait twenty minutes before I come in. Call and let me know where Petrov is sitting, so I can go as far away from him as possible."

"I'll call you," Dillon said, sliding from the driver's seat and heading for the Half Time Rec.

He stepped through the outside door, looked through the inside one and saw Petrov and his three buddies at the far end of the bar. The main length of the bar went straight ahead as you came in the door. It ran most of the length of the room, stopping short of the wall of the men's room, and had a short wing to the right. To the left, the room had tables and chairs and pool tables and a jukebox.

Dillon turned right and moved down the shorter wing of the bar to an open stool near the middle. He ordered a bottle of Grain Belt Premium beer.

As he sat, slowly sipping his beer, he could lean and see the Russians drinking shots of Stolichnaya vodka. After about twenty minutes he called Sonny.

"They are sitting at the far end of the main bar and hitting the vodka pretty hard already. I've got an open stool on my right, and it's out of sight from them. Why don't you come on in."

"Okay. Be there in two shakes."

Chapter Forty-Three

Sonny opened the outside door of the Rec, then quickly looked through the inside one and saw the Russians at the far end of the bar. They didn't seem to be paying attention to the door, so he stepped in and moved to the bar stool on the right side of Dillon.

"They seem to be oblivious to whoever else is in the bar," Sonny said quietly.

"Yeah, other than getting the bartender's attention for another round of shots, they really haven't paid any attention at all to who is in here," Dillon said, turning his head toward Sonny and talking softly so as not to be overheard.

Sonny thanked the bartender for the beer, then leaned toward Dillon, saying, "I think we just let 'em keep drinking. We'll know when the time is right."

About an hour later, the four were ordering their fifth round of the vodka and third round of beer. They were also getting louder and when the bartender brought their latest round, he politely asked them to keep it down a bit. One of Petrov's sidekicks growled at the bartender, "You just shut up and keep bringing vodka."

Petrov slapped him hard in the chest, saying, "You shut up, Ivan. He's nice man, just doing his job."

Ivan raised his hands, saying, "Okay... Okay... I shut up."

Another half hour passed and the Russians were getting louder again, to the point Sonny and Dillon could make out what they were saying. "Let's go to the bar on Rice Street. More women! There's no women in dis place tonight."

Sonny motioned the bartender over. "You're going to have a little trouble in here in a few minutes. We're going to take the leader of those four Russians to the Hennepin County jail. The other three will be littering your floor. Call 9-1-1 right now. Tell them you need police right away... there's a big fight and there may be guns."

Sonny stood from the barstool and slowly moved around the corner of the bar. As he passed the other customers he turned and softly said, "Better step outside for a moment. There's going to be trouble and there may be guns. Don't want anybody to get hurt. It'll only be a minute or two, then you can come back."

The customers quickly and quietly headed toward the door. By the time the Russians noticed, they saw Sonny and Dillon walking up to them. "You again! I owe you one... big time," Petrov said, slamming his beer glass on the bar.

His biggest mistake was expecting Sonny to give him time to turn around and face him and get ready for the fight. Instead, Sonny threw a hard left into Petrov's right temple, leaving him disoriented and queasy, barely able to stay on his feet.

Sonny immediately turned his attention to the one that was to the right of Petrov. When they left their barstools, Sonny told Dillon, "I've got Petrov and the one to the right of him. You got the two on the left." This guy now looked as though he wasn't sure if he was going fight, or try to run.

The instant Dillon saw Sonny throw a punch at Petrov, he hit the bigger of the two on the left with a hard right to the solar plexus. It bent him over and dropped him to one knee, gasping for breath. In a continuous motion, Dillon swung his right forearm toward the other one, who was four or five inches shorter than Dillon, hitting him full in the face. Dillon heard the crunch of bone and figured it was a broken nose. When the guy dropped to his knees holding his face and blood running out between his fingers, he was sure it was a broken nose.

Now, with the other three disabled, the fourth one held his hands nervously out in front and slowly dropped to his knees. Sonny told him, "Face-down on the floor, fingers laced behind your head." Soon, they had Petrov in handcuffs and all three of the others face-down, with fingers laced behind their heads.

Sonny asked the bartender, "Jake, you got any kind of gun behind the bar?"

"No, I don't. But I got this," he held up a large baseball bat and shook it in his fist. "With them face-down on the floor, I think I can keep 'em under control with this till the other cops get here."

"Okay. They should be here in a couple minutes. We're taking this guy downtown."

"Thanks for taking care of this," Jake said, nodding his head, "without wrecking the place in the process."

Sonny and Dillon nodded toward Jake, and hustled Petrov out the door. They wanted to be gone before the police arrived. They didn't have cause to arrest Petrov and didn't want the police to know who took him.

Dillon chained the handcuffs on Petrov to the D-ring bolted to the passenger side floor of his pickup. Then he closed the passenger door and turned to Sonny, who said, "I'll follow you to Ham Lake and worry about bringing this pick-up back to my neighbor tomorrow."

"Okay. We can take Lexington Avenue all the way up to 167th in Ham Lake."

Earlier, Dillon had told Sonny about baby-sitting a friend's home and animals on seven acres in Ham Lake, while they're in Ireland for nearly a month with his consulting company. "There's a pole barn with a heated room that we could keep Petrov in for days until he tells us why he was tailing and harassing Sonja."

Chapter Forty-Four

"Always be content to be what you really are."
Marcus Aurelius (121 – 180 AD)

Dillon drove in to the Ham Lake property and parked by the pole building. He slid from behind the wheel and saw the yellow pickup coming up the drive. He waited for Sonny to park next to him and get out of the truck.

Stepping out and closing the door on the pickup, Sonny said, "Everything go okay?"

"Oh yeah... he was asking me if I knew who we were dealing with. If I knew about the Russian Mafia. I told him to gather up all his friends from the Mafia, and me and Sonny will gather up ours – mine being mostly guys with ultimate fighting backgrounds, and yours being mostly retired special forces guys. I said I was pretty confident it would end up like it did with him and his three buddies against you and me at the Half Time Rec."

Sonny smiled, then gave kind of a silent chuckle, as he slowly shook his head and headed for the passenger door on Dillon's pickup. Petrov glared at Sonny as he opened the pickup's door.

"S-o-o-o," Sonny said, stretching the word. "You're threatening us with the Russian Mafia now." He reached in and opened the padlock holding the chain that looped through the handcuffs and D-ring on the floor. He handed both the lock and the chain to Dillon and asked, "Is the pole barn's door locked... have you got the key?"

"I do," Dillon said and started toward the building.

Sonny reached to take Petrov by the arm. As he did, Petrov jerked his arm away and slid from the pickup seat. A little perturbed, Sonny grabbed the arm and glared at Petrov. "We can do this the easy way," he said nicely, then scowled, "or, if you prefer, we can do it the busted nose way." After that, Petrov seemed to be just a little more cooperative.

Dillon opened the door, turned on the lights and stepped inside. Sonny led Petrov into the room and sat him on a steel office chair.

"This is Bill's tack room and man cave," Dillon said. "So he's got it all insulated and heated. The best thing is that there are still two heavy eye-bolts anchored in the 6 x 6 posts. He would clip his horse's lead rope to them when he brushed them down or whatever. We can chain his leg shackles and handcuffs to those. He won't be going anywhere and no one could hear him yelling from inside this room."

Sonny looked at Petrov, saying, "In case you haven't figured it out yet, we are interested in knowing why you were tailing me a few times, and why you were messing with Sonja at her home."

Petrov stared at the floor a while, then said, "I don't tell you not'ing. People I work for find out and I am dead man."

"You don't seem to understand, Sergei. You're talking about a 'what if' thing, while you're facing reality right here with us. If you don't tell us what we want, you'll be chained to those posts," Sonny said, pointing. "I'm sure you could make it a couple weeks with no food. But, with no water... you'd be lucky to make it three maybe four days."

"Will see," Petrov said, somberly.

"Okay, we'll see. Let's hook him up Dillon."

They clamped shackles around his ankles, then looped a long length of chain through the shackles and the handcuffs, and padlocked the ends of the chain to one of the eyebolts mounted in the 6 x 6 posts. Then they took another long length of chain and looped it through the shackles and handcuffs like the first one, and padlocked the ends of that chain to the eyebolt on the opposite side of the room. This gave Petrov about a foot of slack with which to wiggle around and try to get comfortable.

"Alright Sergei," Sonny said pleasantly, "I'll see you sometime tomorrow afternoon. I'll be bringing dinner for Dillon and me, and probably a six pack of beer. I'll check in with you then. See how you're doing."

Dillon held the door as Sonny walked out, then he clicked the light switch off and closed the door... making sure it was locked.

As they walked toward the pickups, Dillon asked, "Really gonna let him stew in there until tomorrow evening?"

"Might as well," Sonny answered. "I'm betting it takes two days – maybe three – before he'll open up. By then he'll probably have messed himself, and be desperately thirsty."

"You might be right about him not talking after only one day. I'll be staying here most of this week... to take care of things and feed the horses and dogs. I can check on him every couple hours to make sure everything's okay.

"I'll bring dinner for us tomorrow evening, like I said. What'cha hungry for?"

"How about pizza and beer."

"I love the way you think," Sonny said, smiling.

As Sonny left, Dillon was headed for the corral to check the horses. Sonny thought he'd stop on his way home and fill the gas in the yellow pickup so it was ready to return to the neighbor in the morning.

When he finally walked in his house, it was to a nice big hug and kiss from Sonja. "Hello babe," he said sweetly. "How are you?"

"I've been nervous... since you called and said you were taking Petrov up to Ham Lake."

"I told you everything would be okay and I would be home a little late," he said, trying to reassure her.

"Yeah, but you know me... gotta worry."

Chapter Forty-Five

"How strange to be surprised at anything which happens in life."
Marcus Aurelius (121 – 180 AD)

Late the next afternoon, Sonny stopped at Chanticleer Pizza and picked up a large sausage, mushroom and green olive pizza. He knew that was Dillon's favorite and liked it himself as well. Then he swung into a nearby liquor store and bought a six-pack of Grain Belt Premium... another of Dillon's favorites.

He pulled in the drive and, grabbing the pizza and beer, stepped on the porch and rang the doorbell with his elbow. Dillon opened the door and, as though speaking to someone else, shouted, "Pizza man's here!" Grinning, he pushed the screen door open and let Sonny in.

"How's our guest doing?" Sonny asked, as he headed toward the kitchen.

"So far... still stubborn and tight-lipped."

"As we expected," Sonny said, opening the pizza box. "Got any paper plates?

"No, but we can just use these paper towels." Dillon tore off a couple sheets for each of them, then set the roll of paper towels on the counter.

He and Sonny each took a slice of pizza, placed it on the paper towels and moved to the table. Sonny took the six-pack of Grain Belt, set it on the table and took a bottle out for each of them. They each sat in a chair, opened the bottle of beer and began eating pizza.

"Mmmm, delicious!" Dillon said, finishing his first bite and drinking some beer.

After a half hour, the two had finished most of the pizza and their second beer. Sonny suggested they save two small slices of the pizza and the third beer to take with them when they go out to see Petrov. "A little reminder of how thirsty and how hungry he is getting."

The two stepped from the porch and walked across the yard to the pole barn. Dillon unlocked the door and reached in to turn on the light switch. Petrov flinched and squinted his eyes until they slowly became accustomed to the bright lights.

"Sergei Petrov, my friend, how are you doing this evening?" Sonny asked, then took a sip of his beer.

Petrov was not in the mood for talking, especially to these two who were munching pizza and drinking beer. He just glared at Sonny, then at Dillon, then back at the floor.

"Look Sergei," Sonny said, "let me clear this up in case there's some misunderstanding. Just tell us what you wanted with me and Sonja, and we'll take you back to your home and you'll never hear from us again. No harassment... no charges against you... you can fly back to Miami. Fly back to Russia if you want. But you're not going to move from those chains until you tell us something we can believe."

Sonny sat back in his chair, finished the chunk of pizza and drank some beer. Then he looked at Petrov with a shrug that said, *"Well, what ya gonna do Sergei?"*

"Got nothing to say for you," Petrov said, and continued to stare at the floor.

"O-o-k-a-y," Sonny said slowly. "See you tomorrow, then." He rose from his chair and Dillon did the same. As they walked out, Dillon switched the lights off and locked the door once again.

Dillon paused by the Tahoe as Sonny slid in behind the wheel. "Think he'll talk tomorrow?" he asked Sonny.

"Who knows. He may have enough fight in him to make it to the third day. We'll see."

"You may be right. I'll update you in the morning."

"Okay. See you later partner," Sonny said, putting the Tahoe in gear and slowly backing out of the driveway.

He drove south on Lexington, then headed west on Interstate 694 to the Central Avenue exit where he headed south towards his home. As he drove through the Columbia Heights area, his phone rang. He glanced at it and saw that it was Bill Baker calling. He quickly pulled to the curb and answered the call.

"Hello Mr. Baker," he said brightly. Bill Baker was owner of St. Paul Bail Bonds, another client he worked with.

"Hello Sonny," Baker said, "sorry to be calling so late. I've got a pressing need. What's your schedule like?"

Sonny's first thought was, *If any of you in the bail bond business called and didn't have a pressing need, I don't know what I would do.* Instead he said, "My schedule is pretty good. What've you got?"

"A skip that I've got about six weeks left on the calendar. Can you stop by, pick up a copy of the file and tell me what you think?"

"I can do that tomorrow afternoon. How does three o'clock work for you?"

"That works great. Thanks a lot Sonny," Baker said, sounding relieved. Then he said goodbye and hung up his phone.

Sonny dialed Dillon's number and herd, "Hey partner, what's up?"

"I just had a call from Bill Baker. I told him we'd come to his office at three o'clock tomorrow afternoon to talk about a skip he needs help with. Hopefully we'll be done with Petrov by then."

Chapter Forty-Six

"I cannot escape death, but I can escape the fear of it."
Marcus Aurelius (121 – 180 AD)

Late the following morning, Sonny drove in the drive at the Ham Lake property. He'd spoken with Dillon, who said Petrov was looking a little bleak. "He may be ready to talk."

When he pulled in, Dillon came from the corral where he'd been cleaning the horse's hooves and giving them a good brush down. "You should have a property like this," Sonny said, "the way you love animals."

"Yeah, but it's mostly fun when you don't have to do it all the time."

Sonny smiled, looking out at the horses, then asked, "What's the latest on our friend in the barn?"

"I think he's ready to start chatting. He asked if he could have just a little water till you got here."

"Did you give him any?"

Dillon scrunched his face. "N-o-o-o."

"Good. Let's have some lunch. Let him wait."

They walked in the kitchen and Dillon rolled up his sleeves to start making their lunch – Tuna Melt sandwiches. They ate them with sweet pickle slices and potato chips and Dad's old fashioned root beer.

"These sandwiches are delicious," Sonny said. "After all these years, I didn't know you made Tuna Melts."

"One of my specialties," Dillon said, grinning.

"Make one more. We'll bring it out to Petrov, along with two bottles of water from my truck."

"Good thinkin'," Dillon said, and made another one.

They brought the sandwich and two bottles of water out to the barn. They set the food and water on the desk in front of Petrov. Then they each sat down in a chair.

For several minutes neither of them said anything. Petrov just stared at the water. Finally, Sonny said, "Sergei, just tell us what we want to know and you can have the food and the bottles of water. I've even got more water in the truck if you want."

Petrov continued to stare at the water and the food. Sonny and Dillon said nothing for several minutes. Finally Petrov, looking at Sonny, said, "Give me drink of water... I tell you everything."

"You know that's not the way it's going to work," Sonny told him, shaking his head. "You tell us everything and convince us you're telling the truth, and you can have all the water and food you want."

Petrov licked his parched lips and breathed heavily. Finally, after a couple more minutes, he sighed. "You know about Kazakovs? Yes?"

"Yes," Sonny replied, nodding his head.

"I work with them for many years. We steal many valuable paintings, but have no connections to sell them." He rubbed the front of his neck and tried to swallow. "Just a little water, so I can keep talking."

Sonny opened a bottle of water, poured some in a cup and handed it to Petrov. He tipped it back and gulped the water, then closed his eyes enjoying the taste.

"So," Petrov said, continuing, "we hit dead end with no one to sell paintings to. The Kazakovs knew artist – a woman known as 'Lady Pirate' – and they hire her to paint over these treasures and camouflage them. Now they look like nice little paintings worth maybe a couple hundred dollars in art shop.

"Then they track which art shops buy the new paintings and what customers buy them from the shops. Now they know where the masterworks are 'stored.' When they have a buyer willing to pay, they steal painting, remove camouflage and restore original masterwork."

"I don't quite get it," Sonny said. "What does any of this have to do with Sonja or me?"

"Do you remember nice Seascape of Jamaica that Sonja received as gift?"

"Yeah, from a customer she moved. I remember it."

"It's 'Portrait of a Girl' by Gustav Klint. Valued at nearly one million U.S. dollars."

Sonny's eyes opened wide and he looked at Dillon. "Holy..." he started to whisper. "I don't know how you could have made up that story, so I think I believe it. We'll give you all the food water you want, but until I check things out, you're going to stay in those chains. If it turns out the Jamaican seascape is camouflaging a masterwork, I'll keep my word and you'll be free to go. It's the Kazakovs the authorities will want anyway."

Sonny glanced at the clock on the wall, and said, "We better get going. We've got the meeting with Bill Baker at three o'clock."

He grabbed a folding chair, set it in front of Petrov, and put the sandwich and two bottles of water on the chair where he could reach them. "We'll get you two more bottles of water before we leave, and be back in a few hours."

Chapter Forty-Seven

"A thing is neither better nor worse for having been praised."
Marcus Aurelius (121 – 180 AD)

In their meeting with Bill Baker, Baker told them, "This skip's a bad one. Charles 'Lefty' Thompson is up on an 'Armed Robbery' charge and is looking at a possible ten to fifteen. His latest stint was two years in Stillwater, so he's not going to come in willingly."

"You said you had another agent tracking him until a couple weeks ago," Sonny said.

"We did," Baker said. "He tracked him to eastern Arkansas, where Thompson has family. Then to Tennessee where, evidently, he has more family. But Thompson always managed to stay just out of reach. I'm hoping you can do better and in less time."

"Have you got any reports or notes from the other agent? They could be helpful to us."

"Yes, they should be in that file as well," Baker said.

Sonny glanced at Dillon, who gave him a nod that was almost imperceptible. Closing the file, Sonny looked at Baker and said, "I think we can do the job for you. If you want to have your secretary put together a contract while we wait; then we can get going on it tomorrow. With a two hundred thousand dollar bond out on this, any problem with the nineteen percent we charge for risky ones?"

"No, not at this point," Baker said. "Teri should have the contract filled out in about ten minutes."

Leaving Baker's office, Sonny called Sonja at work. "Hi Babe, I'll bet you didn't know you are the owner of a painting worth a million dollars." He glanced at Dillon, who was wearing a big grin.

"What?" she asked, sounding a little flabbergasted. "What are you talking about?"

He explained the scenario Petrov had given them. "According to him, that Seascape of Jamaica your client gave you as a gift is really a hundred-thirty-year-old painting called, 'Portrait of a Girl' by Gustav Klint. And it's worth about one million U.S. dollars."

He listened for a bit and smiled.

"I'm going to pick it up at your place right now and bring it to Adele Dubois at her shop. You remember Adele?"

"Yeah… now she has her own shop and specializes in cleaning and restoration of old works. I'm thinking she should be able to tell us, from the backside or other more scientific way, if the canvas is really over a hundred years old, which it would have to be if it's authentic."

Sonny was listening, smiling and nodding his head. "Yeah, unfortunately, since it's a stolen item, you'll have to return it. Let them pay for the restoration."

"Okay Babe, I'll be back to you as soon as I know more. I probably won't be home until around 8 o'clock. Go ahead and eat dinner if you're hungry. If you want to wait, we can go out for something when I get there."

"Yeah, The Sampler's Corner sounds good. I'm not sure if they take reservations during the week, but why don't you give them a call and see."

He clicked off the call with Sonja and scrolled his contact file for Adele Dubois. Touching the phone icon by her number, he waited for it to ring. He heard her phone ring twice, then a soft voice said, "Adele Dubois."

"Hello Adele, this is Harrison Sawyer... Sonny."

"Well, hello stranger. I haven't seen you in ages, my dear friend."

"Not since the grand opening of your shop a year ago." After a pause, he said, "I need a big favor, Adele."

"What do you need, Sonny?"

He explained in an abbreviated version about Sonja supposedly having "Portrait of a Girl" by Gustav Klint and that it had been painted over to hide it in plain sight. If I bring it to you, is there any way to verify that it's more than a hundred years old? I thought maybe looking at the back of the canvas or something."

"Yes, bring it over. I'm open till nine o'clock tonight. I'm excited to have a look at it. There are a couple of different things I can do to verify if it's new or old."

"Thanks Adele. I'll be there in about an hour."

He said goodbye and hung up the call. "She's excited to see it," he told Dillon.

"It'll be nice if she could give us an answer tonight," Dillon said. "That way we can cut Petrov loose and get after Lefty in Arkansas... or Tennessee... or wherever."

"Assuming it's the real deal, let's plan on giving Petrov a ride home in the early morning. Hopefully, his buddies would still be asleep and we could avoid any confrontation.

They retrieved the painting from Sonja's home and headed to downtown Minneapolis, where Adele's Gallery is near Thirteenth and LaSalle Avenue.

Dillon carried the painting and Sonny held the door to let him in. When Adele saw them, she hurried over and gave Sonny a big hug. After some quick 'hello, how are you' exchanges, Sonny said, "Adele this is my partner Dillon. Dillon... Adele." Dillon handed the painting to Sonny so he could shake her hand. "So glad to meet you," he said.

Adele looked at the painting. "So this is it."

"We're sure hoping it is."

She waved, saying, "Bring it back here and lay it on my work table."

After ten minutes of studying it with a magnifying glass, scratching the frame, and doing a few other things, she said, "Well, I think you're in luck. I think the canvas is more than a hundred years old. The frame is newer to match the 2009 date the camouflage artist put under her signature. They knew what they were doing, too. The Seascape painting can be removed without significantly damaging the original. I'd love to restore it for you."

"I'd love to have you restore it," Sonny said, "but we have to contact the museum it was stolen from first. With any luck they'll commission you to restore it. Until then, can you hold onto it for us? No one will know you have it, and it would be best if we all keep it that way for now."

"I would be glad to hold on to it for you. Even though it's camouflaged, it's the most valuable painting I've ever had in my shop," she said, smiling.

They thanked Adele, said their goodbyes and headed up to the Ham Lake property. "We should bring Petrov something to eat and a few more bottles of water," Sonny said. "I'm going to head back home and take Sonja out to eat. Would you like to stop and pick up something for dinner?"

"Actually, I've got a batch of chicken dumpling soup that my mom sent home with me the other day. I think I'll just heat that up. Sergei and I can have it for supper. Probably be good for him, since he hasn't had solid food for a couple days."

Pulling in the Ham Lake driveway, Sonny said, "I'll grab the rest of the water and give it to Petrov. Let's go let him know that he will be free in the morning, and that we'll give him a ride back to his house in St. Paul.

Dillon unlocked the door and switched on the light. Petrov squinted his eyes, as before, until they gradually got used to the bright light. Sonny set the case of bottled water – the remaining eleven bottles anyway – on the folding chair in front of Sergei.

"It looks like we'll be setting you free in the morning and giving you a ride to your home in St. Paul. My friend that restores old works of art is convinced that 'Portrait of a Girl' is under the Jamaican seascape. We'll be contacting the museum that you and the Kazakovs stole it from.

"My advice is that you get out of Minnesota... head back to Florida... head back to Russia for all I care. But if we cross paths with you again, it won't end well for you. And you're going to have to deal with the Kazakovs... figure out what story you'll tell them."

Sergei Petrov just listened and nodded.

The next morning they drove Petrov back to his home. As hoped, everyone in the St. Paul house was asleep when they arrived. They watched Petrov knock for several minutes, until finally someone answered the door.

As they drove away, Dillon asked, "Think he'll take your advice and leave Minnesota?"

"Who knows? We can only hope."

Chapter Forty-Eight

"Don't dwell on what you lack, rather be thankful for what you have."
Marcus Aurelius (121 – 180 AD)

The next day at Sonny's home, they began dissecting the file of Charles "Lefty" Thompson. First item in Sonny's notes was that his mother, Emma Thompson, still lived at 224 Lee St., Earle, Arkansas. Sonny turned to his computer and printed out detailed maps of Arkansas, the city of Earle, and Crittenden County where Earle is located.

Next they found that Thompson's sister, Cheryl Randall, lives at 3727 Cedar St., Fisherville, Tennessee. Again, Sonny printed maps of Tennessee, the city of Fisherville, and Shelby County.

"His ex-wife lives in Columbia, Missouri," Dillon said, looking up at Sonny. "We may have crossed her path when we were dealing with Little Johnny from St. Louis."

Sonny grinned, then said, "So far nothing jumps out as a place to start with Thompson."

"The notes from the previous agent seem to indicate that he spent a fair amount of time at his mother's place. Maybe we start with her," Dillon said with a shrug.

"That's probably as good as we've got. How about some "Dagwood" sandwiches for lunch and think on it?"

"Your turn for making sandwiches?" Dillon asked.

"Yup. Want onions on yours?"

"Yes Sir, I'll take the works."

After lunch, they decided Emma Thompson in Earle, Arkansas was the best place to start. Sonny suggested he talk to Saul Berkowitz and see if they could hire Chris for a couple hours. "See if he can get any phone records for Thompson, his mother, and his sister Cheryl."

Saul agreed to their proposal, at a rate of seventy-five dollars per hour for Chris's time. Saul said, "Use him as many hours as you need tomorrow."

"Thanks, so much," Sonny said. "I really appreciate the help."

Shortly after eight o'clock the next morning, they were headed to Saul's office to meet with Chris. They parked in the ramp across the street and walked to the door that read Midwest Bail Bonds in bold white lettering.

After the usual bit of friendly flirting with Deb, she said, "Chris told me you were coming in this morning. He's at his desk... go on back."

Chris was ready for them, with two folding chairs leaning against his desk. As they neared, he said, "Grab a chair, fellas." As they opened the chairs and sat, he reached for a legal pad on his desk and picked up his pen. "So, who is it I'm going to be finding records on?"

"The guy's name is Charles Thompson," Sonny said. "His last known phone number was 507-626-3939. See if you can come up with the last five or six months on that number and, maybe more importantly, any other numbers that are in Thompson's name.

"Next is his mother, Emma Thompson. She lives at 224 Lee Street, Earle, Arkansas.

"His sister is Cheryl Randall, and she lives at 3727 Cedar Street in Fisherville, Tennessee. Everything that we can get on mom and sis would be great, too."

"That's it?" Chris asked.

"If you can get stuff on those three, that would be fantastic," Sonny told him.

"Well... shouldn't be too tough," Chris said, looking at his notes. Then looking up from the notes he said, "Why don't you give me an hour. Go have breakfast or something. I should have what you need when you get back."

Sonny and Dillon looked at each other, a little surprised. "Okay then," Sonny said. "See you in an hour."

Back out on the sidewalk, Dillon said, "Why don't we walk over to Bob's Breakfast Corner? It's just a couple blocks away, and he has great coffee."

"Sounds good. I had a light breakfast early this morning, so I might even be up for an omelet or something."

They both ordered the Western Omelet and drank a couple cups of Bob's coffee... his 'Special Brew.' Almost an hour later, they were walking back to Saul's office.

"I wonder how much Chris was able to find on Thompson and his family?" Dillon asked.

"Hopefully lots," Sonny said. "We'll know in just a couple minutes."

Walking in the door, smiling and saying, "Hello again", as they passed Deb's desk, they headed back to Chris's desk – both anxious to see what he had found.

"I found lots of interesting things," Chris told them as they sat. "First is, the number you gave me for Thompson is still working and I've got the last five months detailed." As he said this, he flashed them the report and laid it on his desk.

"Second, I found working phone numbers for Emma and Cheryl. Here are the reports on them." Again, he quickly showed the reports and laid them on the first one.

"Third, I found a strange quirk in these reports. Charles' first phone, the cell phone with area code 507, showed regular calls to his mom, Emma, and occasional calls to his sister, Cheryl, until three months ago when they stopped. That's when he got a new phone with a 901 area code. From that point on, there were no calls to his mom or sister on *either phone*. AND, there were no calls from Emma's or Cheryl's phones to the 507 number. Very strange... no calls between the three of them at all starting three months ago, the same time he got the new cell phone.

Sonny and Dillon sat quietly listening to Chris; both a little surprised, and both very impressed.

"Forth, I started back tracing the calls on the new cell phone with the 901 area code, which is the area code for most of Memphis. I could only identify the callers on about one third of all the calls made or received. About three fourths of the unknown calls were to one number, and the other fourth to another number.

"My conclusion: Since all calls between Thompson, his mother, and his sister ended at the same time... that he purchased a new phone for himself, and 'burners' for each of them so there'd be no record of calls. That way they could call each other with little fear of somebody tracking them.

"Finally, his new cell phone shows regular calls to one number, probably mom's burner, and occasional calls to another number, probably his sister's burner, and they originate somewhere around the Memphis area. Earle, Arkansas, is a half hour west of Memphis. Fisherville, Tennessee, is a half hour east, so Thompson is likely in the Memphis area."

He quickly showed Sonny and Dillon these last reports and placed them on the others. "I'll make copies of these for each of you," he said, gathering them up and squaring them up in his hands.

Sonny sat quietly staring at Chris for a moment. "That's impressive, Chris. Very impressive."

Standing from his desk chair, Chris showed a smile and said, "Thanks, Sonny. I'll be right back with your copies."

Chapter Forty-Nine

*"A rock is thrown in the air. It gained nothing by going up.
It loses nothing by coming down."*
Marcus Aurelius (121 – 180 AD)

The following morning, Sonny and Dillon were packed and on the road at 5:30 AM. They hoped to be in Memphis and checked in to a motel room by 6:30 PM. The plan was to start in Earle, Arkansas, with surveillance on Emma Thompson, Lefty's mother. Depending on how things developed, they talked about splitting up and having one watching Emma and the other watching Cheryl in Fisherville, Tennessee.

"We've got a room with two queen beds at the Quality Suites right off Interstate 55," Dillon said, looking at a map of Memphis. "So we'll be about a half hour away from both Fisherville and Earle. We have a ground-level room where we can park the Tahoe right in front of the door and bring all of our gear inside."

"Sounds good." Sonny said, pausing in thought. "I was thinking about Thompson last night... until I finally drifted off to sleep. My guess is he's staying in some little place outside Memphis that's off the grid."

"I'd say you're right," Dillon said. "If it were me, that's what I would be doing."

"But, I guess it doesn't matter until we find a way to locate him and get cuffs on him."

"Like you've taught me, it's just putting your boots on the ground and see where the leads take you."

They checked in at the Quality Suites a half-hour ahead of schedule that evening. After unloading the Tahoe, they decided to take a quick run out to Earle, Arkansas, to get the lay of the land under the cover of darkness.

In Earle, they drove down Lee Street, slowly passing Emma's little house. "With any luck," Sonny said, "this cabinet shop across the street will have a few of the worker's cars in the parking lot. We could park in there and not look too conspicuous. And it's a couple houses down from hers."

"Conspicuous is the right word," Dillon said. "It looks like the cabinet shop is the only place where we wouldn't stick out like strangers."

"That's where we'll start in the morning, then. We'll have to go in and talk to the owner and give him a reason why we're going to be sitting in his parking lot."

"I think flashing our IDs and telling him we're Federal Agents, and that we need his help... mostly by him not saying a word to anyone who we are or why we're doing surveillance from his parking lot. Keep it simple," Dillon said.

Sonny nodded. "Now, let's go see if The Tennessee Roadhouse near the motel is any good."

Walking in the door, the Roadhouse looked very interesting and they decided to stay for drinks and dinner. The waitress was attractive, intelligent and had a good sense of humor. She brought their drinks and asked if they were ready to order food.

"I'll have the T-bone, medium rare, with a baked potato and blue cheese dressing on my salad," Dillon said.

"I'll have exactly the same," Sonny said, smiling.

A little past eight o'clock the next morning, Sonny and Dillon were at the Crittenden County Sheriff's office in West Memphis, Arkansas, to explain the reason for them being in their county, and that they intended to apprehend Charles Thompson and bring him back to Minnesota. The deputy they spoke with assured them the cooperation of the Sheriff's office. He asked, "Could I have a business card so we have your number, just in case we come across anything that might be helpful to you?"

"Sharp deputy," Dillon said, as they climbed back in the Tahoe and headed for the little town of Earle.

"Yes he is. Refreshing. Not a word I would usually use, but that's what came to mind."

They pulled in the parking lot of "Bill Lee's Cabinet Shop," across from Emma Thompson's little home. They walked inside hoping Bill Lee was in that morning. He was, and his secretary/receptionist/order taker called for him over the loudspeaker. In a couple of minutes, a man walked up with his hand extended, saying, "I'm Bill. How can I help you gentlemen?"

Sonny shook his hand, saying, "I'm Sonny and this is Dillon. You were recommended to do the cabinetry for our office building in Memphis. Could you show us around your shop and some of your finished work?"

"I'd be happy to. Follow me."

As they walked away, Sonny quickly scanned the area and, seeing no one within earshot, said, "Could you hold up just a sec, Bill."

Looking from Sonny to Dillon, he asked, "Yes?"

"Actually," Sonny said, quickly showing Bill his identification, "I just wanted to get you away from others so they wouldn't overhear. We're federal agents. We have an arrest warrant and are in pursuit of a man who is wanted in Minnesota. We hoped it would be okay with you if we parked in your lot to do surveillance. We have a couple of spots here, in Memphis, and in Fisherville Tennessee where we will be doing surveillance of local homes hoping to find this guy."

"I've got no problem with that. I appreciate you letting me know. What should I tell my employees if anyone asks what you're doing here... in our parking lot?"

"As little as possible. Keep it simple. Maybe just say you have an appointment later to come and look at our offices."

"No problem. I'll figure something out."

Sonny shook his hand, saying, "Thanks so much, Bill." He was a slight man – maybe 5' 7" and 140 pounds – but Sonny noticed the firm handshake and his obvious arm and hand strength. *Probably from decades of working with his hands*, he thought.

They returned to the Tahoe and got comfortable for a long day watching Emma's home. Sonny checked the Nikon binoculars and Dillon was checking the Canon digital camera that has a telephoto lens. They set these on the console between them and Dillon reached for water and a snack bar.

"Want some?" he asked Sonny.

"Sure."

"Here," Dillon said, handing them to Sonny and reaching back for more.

As is usually the case with surveillance, the day was long and slow, with little activity at Emma's home. By mid-afternoon, Sonny said, "I think we should rent a car in the morning, stop at the Shelby County Sheriff's office, then go see about surveillance at his sister's place in Fisherville.

"After that, we can split the duties like we talked about and double our coverage."

"Good strategy," Dillon said. "I think we should rent a pickup or a Jeep. That way we won't stand out quite so much. With some of the rental cars, you might as well have a sign hanging on it that says, 'I'm a stranger in your neighborhood.'"

Sonny chuckled. "Yeah, you're probably right."

Dillon grabbed his phone and looked online for car rentals in Memphis. "There's an Enterprise rental office a half mile from the motel," he said, dialing their number.

Sonny overheard him reserving a Jeep. Dillon clicked off the call and said, "We can pick it up any time after seven in the morning."

"We might as well drive that out to Fisherville tomorrow," Sonny said. "Get use to the vehicle."

By late afternoon, when they thought the workers would be leaving for the day, they drove out of the parking lot, around the town of Earle and back toward Emma's home. They parked down the street about four houses away, hoping they wouldn't be noticed.

By 9:15 that evening, the lights were out in her home. Only a nightlight in one room, probably the bathroom, gave light to the window shade.

"Don't think Lefty is going to be visiting mom at this hour," Dillon said.

Turning the key to start the Tahoe, Sonny said, "Good night, Emma."

Dillon just grinned.

Chapter Fifty

"It's silly to try to escape the faults of others. Just try to escape your own."
Marcus Aurelius (121 – 180 AD)

The next morning, Sonny and Dillon decided to walk to Enterprise Rentals for some exercise, since it was only half-mile from the motel. They rented the Jeep, and Dillon drove them back to the motel to get their equipment, food and water for a stakeout. They stopped at the Shelby County Sheriff's office to check in with them, then they drove to Fisherville and found Cheryl's house on Cedar Street.

Down the street a half block, on the opposite side of the street, was a small Baptist Church. "Their parking lot would be the spot for surveillance," Dillon said, pointing.

"Yes, it would, and for now I don't think we need to talk to anybody about parking there. Potential church members... something like that."

"Something like that?" Dillon asked, chuckling. He pulled the Jeep into the lot and swung around to a parking space that faced Cheryl's home. They both checked out the home with the binoculars and the Canon camera with a telephoto lens.

"We've got a blind spot at the service door to the garage," Sonny said, "but that shouldn't matter because we've got a good view of the overhead door."

"When we drove by, I noticed a large deck in back. Can't see that from here either... not a big deal though."

They both settled back in their seat and got comfortable for the stakeout.

Over the next four or five hours, they snacked on fruit bars and drank water. Dillon leaned forward in his seat and pointed. "I've been noticing a piece of that Dairy Queen sign a few blocks over. I think I'll walk over there and get a burger and fries and Pepsi. How about you?"

"Yeah, I guess I'll take whatever they've got for a cheeseburger meal."

Dillon opened his door, swung out, stood and stretched for a few moments. Then he hiked over to the DQ, ordered two deluxe cheeseburger meals and sodas, then hiked back to the Jeep.

He handed a deluxe cheeseburger and fries to Sonny, then put his soda and one of the cup holders in the console. Then he handed him several napkins. Spreading his own napkins on his lap, he opened the cheeseburger, spread out the rapper, and dumped the fries next to the burger. "Ahhhh, the wonderful world of fast food," he said, sarcastically, then munched on a couple of french fries.

Almost done with his food, Sonny was sipping on the soda. He stopped, stared, then said, "Bogey at two o'clock."

Dillon quickly looked up from his food, turning to look down the street. A car was slowing as it neared Cheryl's driveway. The guy behind the wheel vaguely resembled the photos they had of Thompson. "Is that him?"

Sonny nodded his head. "Think so."

The car pulled in the drive and when the driver got out, Dillon said, "Looks like the right size... fits the profile... looks a little like the photos... must be him."

Again, Sonny nodded his head, saying, "Think so."

The driver, presumably Thompson, walked toward the back of the house. After a couple minutes, Sonny said, "Must have gone on that deck we can't see and in the back door."

"Whad'aya think? Should we try and take him?" Dillon asked, staring at the house.

"Y-e-a-h... let's give him a couple minutes first. Figure out what we want to do."

They waited a few minutes, then they both perked up and looked at each other. "See that?" Dillon asked.

"Yup, I did." Someone had pulled back the curtain a bit and looked out the front window. "He may have spotted us. I think we better move on him... now," Sonny said, drawing his Glock to check it before he got out. Dillon did the same, then they hurried to Cheryl's yard.

"You want the front or the back?" Sonny asked Dillon.

"I'll take the back and wait by the deck until I hear something."

"Okay. Be careful, partner."

Sonny waited a few beats to give Dillon time to get around back, then he climbed the front steps and knocked on the door. He waited about twenty seconds and knocked on the door again, this time much louder. Finally, after a few more seconds, he knocked and shouted, "We know you're in there Thompson. Open the door."

He tried the doorknob on the off chance that it was unlocked. No such luck. It was locked up tight... probably the deadbolt, too. He was ready to shout again, when he heard gunshots coming from the back of the house.

He hurried around the side where Dillon had gone, looking everywhere for him, his Glock held in both hands in front of him and pointing everywhere he looked. "Dillon?" He shouted, checking all around the deck area.

He circled around the deck toward the far side of the house and saw Dillon's body, bloody and lifeless. When he moved toward the body, he quickly checked the back door and window. Through the storm door he saw movement, aimed the Glock and fired. Seeing no more movement, he knew he had either hit his mark or the guy ducked away.

He hurried to Dillon and his heart sank when he saw all the blood and no movement. He gently placed the fingers of his left hand on the side of Dillon's neck, feeling for the carotid artery and a pulse.

Instantly, Sonny was excited and tapping the side of Dillon's face saying, "Dillon... Dillon... come on buddy, stay with me."

Quickly, he looked up to be sure there was no one at the back door or window, then turned his attention back to Dillon. "Come on buddy," he said lightly slapping the side of Dillon's face. "Stay with me buddy... don't let go... don't you dare let go."

Dillon coughed, then turned his head and coughed some more. "That's it buddy," Sonny said. "That's it. Cough it out so you can breathe."

Dillon groaned, then coughed again.

"Can you hear me Dillon?" Sonny asked.

Through the choking and coughing, he could hear Dillon say, "Y-e-a-h... can hear y-o-u."

Sonny raised Dillon up to a sitting position, and propped him against the corner post of the deck. Then he grabbed Dillon's gun, shook the dirt off it and checked it to be sure there was a round in the chamber.

He placed the gun in Dillon's hand, saying, "I'm going to yank some wires on Thompson's car so he can't get away. Then I'm running to the Jeep to call 9-1-1 and get our first aid kit."

Dillon weakly nodded, as though he understood. "Go," he whispered.

Sonny checked the back door and window again, then ran around to Thompson's car and opened the driver's door. With his left hand he grabbed a bunch of the wires under the dash near the steering wheel, while his right hand fished the knife from his pocket. Slicing all the wiring he could get at, he turned and sprinted toward the Jeep.

After calling 9-1-1 requesting police help and an ambulance, he grabbed their first aid kit and ran back to Dillon. When he got to him, Dillon's eyes were closed. "You okay buddy? You still with me?"

His eyes didn't open, but Sonny was relieved when he heard, "M-m-m h-m-m-m."

Sonny opened a bottle of water and soaked a large gauze pad. He began cleaning the blood from Dillon's head, trying to see where and how bad the wound was. It appeared a bullet had grazed his skull and tore off a chunk of scalp. The bleeding, which had stopped, was reopened a bit with Sonny's cleaning. Sonny folded a small piece of gauze, placed it on the wound and wrapped Dillon's head with the long, rolled up strip of gauze.

Next, Sonny tore open Dillon's shirt to check the wound in his left shoulder. He grabbed the biggest piece of gauze, soaked it with water and began cleaning his shoulder and chest. There was lots of blood and the wound was still bleeding. He rinsed the gauze and put it back on the wound, saying, "Dillon, can you press on this?"

Dillon reached in with his right hand and pressed on the gauze. Then he weakly asked Sonny, "Do I have to do all the work?"

As Sonny reached for his knife, to cut the back of Dillon's shirt open, he said, "Why do you think you get paid the big money."

The exit wound looked pretty clean, with no bone fragments, so Sonny thought it must have been a good through and through. As good as you can hope for anyway, with a gun wound like this.

"Looks like you'll make it just fine," Sonny said.

"Easy for you to say," Dillon groaned.

Chapter Fifty-One

"Nothing happens to anyone that he can't endure."
Marcus Aurelius (121 – 180 AD)

Sonny looked toward the street after catching a glimpse of flashing lights in front of the house. It was an ambulance and a squad car. He had asked them to come without sirens and they had complied.

"Hold tight, partner. I'm going to talk to the police and the paramedics. Be right back," Sonny said, patting Dillon on his good shoulder.

He told the paramedics, "My partner is around this way and leaning against the corner post of the deck. He took a bullet through his shoulder and one grazed the side of his head." The paramedics rushed around the corner of the house and Sonny turned his attention to the police officers, explaining why he and Dillon were in Fisherville, and their intention to bring Charles Thompson back to Minnesota.

"Did Thompson shoot your partner?" one of the officers asked.

"Either he did, or whoever is in there with him did."

"I'll take the back door," the officer said. "You," pointing at Sonny, "follow my partner through the front door. No knocking, just shout a warning then kick it in."

The officer hurried around the house toward the back door and Sonny followed the other officer to the front door. Pausing briefly, he heard the first officer on the radio saying, "Going in."

With that, the officer at the front door shouted, "Police officers... we're coming in." He stepped back, then lunged at the door kicking it hard next to the door knob. The wood of the door and the doorframe cracked, but didn't give way. He planted a second kick and the door flew open. With his gun held in both hands in front of him, he quickly scanned the room. "Are you in, Liam?" he shouted.

"In the kitchen... kitchen is clear," he shouted back.

One by one, all the rooms of the main level were checked and cleared. Then Liam said, "I'll check the basement. You guys check upstairs."

Sonny followed the officer up the stairway where they checked the two bedrooms, a small bathroom, and a small sitting room. They found no one. They headed back down to the living room where they found Liam opening the front curtains. He looked up and down the street then turned to Sonny, asking, "Do you think this guy could have slipped away while you were helping your partner?"

"Yeah, he could have gotten away on foot. I disabled his car and that's still in the driveway."

"Well, that seems like it would be the most likely scenario, since we can't find anybody in the house."

Sonny noticed the paramedics carrying Dillon toward the ambulance, and held up a finger saying, "I'm going to run and talk to my partner before they haul him away."

The paramedics were just getting ready to lift Dillon into the back of the ambulance when Sonny shouted, "Hold up just a second, please." As he neared, he asked, "Where will you be bringing him?"

"Baptist Memorial Hospital near Collierville," one of the paramedics answered.

"I'll be there in a couple hours to check on you," he told Dillon. "Don't be giving them fits at the hospital."

Dillon showed a little grin and said, "See you later."

Sonny headed back into the living room where one of the officers was making notes in a tablet; presumably for the report he would have to write later.

He asked, "What is your full name, Sonny?"

"Harrison Lee Sawyer Junior," he told him.

"And your home address?"

He told him.

"And what is your partner's full name?"

"Dillon Bishop."

"No middle name?" the officer wondered.

Sonny shook his head. "No middle name."

While the officer was getting his information for his report, Sonny was admiring the 'library,' the elaborate shelving built into the wall between the living room and the dining room. It was very classy and filled with books and memorabilia.

As he stood admiring the beautiful woodwork and craftsmanship, he remembered there was a built-in hutch on the other side of that wall. He was right. On the dining room side there was a hutch built with the same beautiful woodwork and craftsmanship.

One of the officers was admiring them as well, and said, "Can you imagine the cost of having that kind of work done in a new home today."

Sonny just smiled, as he slowly shook his head. "An arm and a leg... if you could find the cabinet builder who can do that kind of work."

As he walked back toward the living room, something struck Sonny as not quite right about the wall and the shelves. As he moved around the wall that had the sets of shelves built in on either side, he stopped. First he leaned to the right and looked at the library shelves, then he took a couple short steps and leaned to the left and looked at the hutch shelves. Then he stepped back from the end of the wall, looking and trying to make sense of it in his mind

"What's wrong?" the officer asked.

"Not sure," Sonny said. "Something's not adding up just right." He held up a finger as though asking them to hold on for a minute.

He walked around to the living room side and looked at the library shelving again. Then he walked around the dining room side and looked at the hutch shelving. Then he looked at the end of the wall, spreading his arms to the approximate with of that wall space.

I'll bet there's a small 'safe space' built in there, he thought to himself.

He looked at the two officers, held a finger to his lips to indicate quiet, then waved for them to follow him to the kitchen. In the kitchen, he spoke softly saying, "I think Thompson may be in there."

"In where?" Liam, the older officer, asked.

"In the space between the library shelves in the living room and the hutch shelves in the dining room. If you look at the end wall of that space, it's a little over six feet wide. The shelving on each side is barely over a foot deep. Why build it so you're wasting four feet of space in between?"

Both officers looked at him warily. Then Liam said, "I think you've watched too many old movies."

"Maybe so, but still there's four feet of space between those shelves. I think it's worth trying to see if there's a way to get in there."

A little skeptical, Liam said, "Okay, let's look."

Sonny grabbed his arm as he headed toward the hutch. "Let's be quiet as we can, don't even talk. If he panics, he could start randomly shooting through the shelves and through the wall. We don't need that. You two check the hutch. Look for any kind of latch or release that could swing the unit open. I'll check the library side."

They quietly moved and started their search. The two officers looked everywhere around the hutch shelves and the trim boards, looking for anything unusual.

Sonny did the same in the living room, looking in and under all the shelving and around all the trim work. The top trim board was seven and a half feet off the floor, but he could easily reach it and slowly moved his fingers along the top edge. About a foot from the right corner of the shelving, there was a large notch cut into the heavy trim board. Not sure of just what he was feeling, he decided to pull a nearby chair over and stand on it to have a look.

Before doing that, he quietly walked around the other side and waved for the two officers to join him. In the living room pointing at the top corner of the library shelving, he whispered, "There's a large groove cut into the top of that trim board. I'm going to get on that chair that I moved to the side of the shelving and have a look. Be ready."

They each drew their weapon and moved a little closer to the library shelving. Sonny stepped up on the chair and leaned to look at the notch in the top trim

The notch in the board was about a half inch wide, an inch deep, and about eight inches long. In it was a steel rod that looked like it was hinged on a pin at the left end, with enough space to grab it on the right end and lift up. *Gotta be a latch of some kind,* he thought.

He stepped down from the chair, drew his Glock, and whispered, "Here we go."

He reached up, felt the lever and lifted on the right end. He heard something that sounded like a latch opening. He immediately shouted, "Thompson, there's three of us out here with weapons. You want a war; I think you'll be on the losing side."

Sonny was surprised by the ease with which the shelving swung open. Inside were Thompson and his sister, Cheryl, sitting on small chairs with their hands raised. "If it wasn't for my little sis here," Thompson said, tilting his head toward his sister, "I would have started that war."

Liam waved his gun, motioning them out of the space. "You're under arrest. Please turn around and put your hands behind you." As Liam put cuffs on the two, his partner read them their Miranda rights.

After Lefty and Cheryl were put in the back seat of the squad car, Sonny said, "I'll be down with my paperwork to pick him up and bring him back to Minnesota. If they could just put him in a holding cell for a couple hours that would be great."

He shook the officers hands saying, "Thanks you guys. I really appreciate all your help."

"Thank you," Liam said. "I'm tellin' you, I've been wearing this badge for thirty-two years and have never seen better detective work. Your nickname should be Sherlock."

"Just got lucky," Sonny said with a shrug. "Thanks again, guys." He turned and walked toward the Jeep, thinking he needed to call and get directions to the Baptist Memorial Hospital.

He got directions to take Interstate 269 south to Highway 72, then west to the hospital. Along the way, he dialed Sonja's number. It rang, then he heard her sweet voice saying, "Well, hello handsome. How are you?"

"I'm great," he said softly, "now that I'm in the comfort of your sweet voice."

"Oh my... you smooth talker you." Then she asked, "What's up with you guys today? Any leads on getting your man yet?"

"We got our man! Should be home in a couple days."

"Couple days? If you've got him, why would it take you a couple days to get home?"

"Minor problem along the way. Dillon took a bullet in his shoulder and one grazed his head, too."

"O-h-h n-o-o-o," she cried out. "Minor problem? Being shot is not a minor problem, Sonny."

"He's doing good," Sonny told her. "I'm on my way to the hospital to see him right now."

"Well, okay then. But stop with the 'understatement' on everything. It's gonna drive me crazy."

"Okay Babe, I'll try. We've had this debate before. You know I don't like everything treated like it's some big, end of the world, drama."

"I know... I'm sorry. Just caught me by surprise. But Dillon is doing good?

"Yup. He was doing good before the ambulance even took him away. Would you call Vicki and let her know. You can do it better than I can."

"Sure. I'll do that. What hospital is he at?"

He told her the Baptist Memorial Hospital and gave her the phone number. "I'll call you back with an update after I visit him."

Chapter Fifty-Two

"Imagine you're dead. Now see the rest of your life as a bonus."
Marcus Aurelius (121 – 180 AD)

At the hospital, Dillon was telling Sonny what he remembered prior to getting shot. "I was circling the deck, trying to see any movement from inside the back of the house. When I got around to the far side of the deck, I heard a loud gunshot from my right. I ducked, then looked and saw a puff of smoke on the ground. I think someone threw a cherry bomb or firecracker to distract me... and it worked.

"While I'm looking at the smoke, I hear the screen door squeak and turned back to see what's up. By the time I did that, Thompson was already aiming and shooting. I felt the first bullet hit me high in my chest... burned like hell!

"The last thing I remember is something hitting me in the head. It must've knocked me out."

"Well, I think you know now, don't you," Sonny said. "That last thing was another bullet that grazed your skull and did knock you out. Thankfully, it didn't do worse."

"Then, I guess, the next thing I remember was waking up with you slapping my face."

Sonny chuckled, then said, "And that pretty much brings us up to date. What are the doctors telling you?"

"They're telling me I'm a very lucky guy... as if I didn't know that," he said, rolling his eyes.

"Now be nice," Sonny scolded.

"The doctor told me they put a few stitches in my chest and back to close up the wounds, and said that everything looks pretty good. They're hoping to release me by lunch tomorrow."

"That's good! I think I'll get everything ready to head back to Minnesota when I pick you up here tomorrow. We can drive about halfway in the afternoon, get a comfortable room tomorrow night, then travel the other half of the trip on the following day. No sense trying to push through in one long stretch.

"Sounds good to me," Dillon said. "I'd just like to get home and have Vicki pamper me for a couple days."

Sonny left the hospital and brought the Jeep back to Enterprise Rentals, and they gave him a ride back to the motel. He called the Shelby County Jail and, after talking to several people, finally spoke to an officer who was aware of Charles Thompson's status.

"I will be there tomorrow between noon and one o'clock to pick up Thompson," Sonny told him. "I'll have the necessary paperwork with me."

"Yes, that'll be great," he told the deputy.

He clicked off the call, wondering about Thompson and a motel room. In all his years working as a skip tracer, he'd never held a skip in a motel room overnight. He wasn't worried about it though... he knew they'd figure something out to make sure Thompson was secured.

Sonny picked up his phone and called Sonya to update her on Dillon's condition. He heard her phone ring and, when she answered, he heard, "Well, it's nice to hear from you so soon again, handsome."

He smiled and said, "Just wanted to let you know that Dillon was doing great, and that they will be releasing him tomorrow. I'll be picking him up about noon and we'll head for Minnesota."

"That's great news. I'll call Vicki and let her know, in case she hasn't heard that from Dillon yet."

"I think we're just gonna go halfway tomorrow afternoon and get a motel. We'll travel the second half the next morning and should have Dillon at his home by early afternoon, after we drop Thompson at the Ramsey County jail. What time do you think you'll be home from work tomorrow evening?"

"I can't wait that long," she said. "I think I'll take a long lunch and meet you guys at Dillon's house with Vicki. That way I can say hello to Dillon, and to you. Then I'll be home – back to your house – from work probably about six o'clock."

"That'll be great," he said. "Can't wait to see you."

Two days later, at 12:45 PM, they were checking Charles Thompson into the Ramsey County jail in downtown St. Paul. After completing all the necessary paperwork, they climbed back in the Tahoe and headed for Dillon's home. As they turned on Dillon's street, they saw both Vicki and Sonja's cars parked in front of his home. He pulled the Tahoe up to the curb and the two women ran from the front door to greet them.

Vicki helped Dillon from the Tahoe, asking, "How you doing, sweetie?"

"I'm doing great, hun."

She hugged him gently, then she kissed him all over his face.

At the same time, Sonja gave Sonny a big hug and a sensuous kiss on the lips. "Mmmm, good to see you," she whispered softly.

"Good to see you, too, and feel those luscious lips."

Then Sonja turned to Dillon. "Sure glad to see you, Dillon. Glad to see your doing so well."

He smiled and nodded, and they all headed for his front door.

Next morning, Sonny slept in and didn't get out of bed until 8:30 AM. After his usual morning rituals and a light breakfast, he headed out to Bill Baker's office. He had phoned Bill when they left Memphis, saying, "We should be turning Thompson over to the Ramsey County by about noon tomorrow. I'll be at your office the following morning with the paperwork and pick up our check."

As he backed out of his garage and turned onto the street, he pulled to the curb for a moment to call Baker's office. He punched in the number, heard it ring, then heard the receptionist's voice saying, "St. Paul Bail Bonds, how may I help you?"

"Hi Leslie, this is Sonny. Is Bill of available?"

"No, sorry Sonny. He's meeting with a new client and the client's attorney."

"That's okay. I'm on my way with the paperwork for Charles Thompson. Hopefully Bill has a check written and ready for us."

"Okay, Sonny, I look forward to seeing you and will make sure we have a check ready for you. I'm going right in, interrupt their meeting and see if Bill has the check."

Sonny laughed, said good bye and clicked off the call. He laid his phone on the passenger seat, put the Tahoe in drive and turned south on Central Avenue. Then he headed east on University and on to downtown St. Paul.

At Baker's office, he stepped in the door to a big, "Hi Sonny, how are you?" from Leslie.

"I'm doing great. And I'll be even better if you tell me you've got a check for me."

She smiled, waving a check at him and reaching out toward him with it.

Sonny stepped forward, took the check from her and smiled. "Made my day!" he said.

"Hold on one second, Sonny. Bill wanted to thank you personally." She picked up the phone, pressed Bill's number on the intercom system and said, "Sonny's here with the paperwork for Thompson."

She hung up the phone and looked at Sonny. "He'll be right out."

Baker came out of his office wearing a big smile. He reached out toward Sonny and shook his hand vigorously. "I can't believe you rounded the guy up in a week. Sometimes you amaze me."

Sonny shrugged his shoulders, saying, "I've been on a good lucky streak this past couple months. Sometimes that's all it takes."

He left St. Paul and headed for Dillon's home. He planned to stop at Shaw's to pick up his partners favorite burger and fries and something for himself to eat. Vicki was unable to get the day off at work and be with Dillon, so Sonny thought he would bring him lunch and visit for a while. Maybe check to see if he needed the dressings changed on his wounds or if there was anything else he could do.

Chapter Fifty-Three

"Be tolerant with others and strict with yourself."
Marcus Aurelius (121 – 180 AD)

Dillon seemed to be in a particularly good mood when Sonny walked in with lunch from Shaw's. "You must be one of them there psychedelics," he told Sonny. "Reading my mind and knowing that I was hungry for a Sunburger."

"No, I just knew you'd be hungry for a good burger."

"Same thing," Dillon said, shrugging his shoulders. He led the way to the kitchen, grabbed some napkins, then sat in his usual chair at the table. Sonny knew where his usual chair was, and had taken a seat in the one across from it.

"You look like you're doing pretty well," Sonny said. "You're quite the site though, with the bandage around your head and your arm in a sling."

"Yeah, I do look like a sight, but feel pretty good. The pain pills the doctor gave me are little on the mild side, but enough to dull the pain so that I don't notice it much."

"How long did the doctor say you needed to lay low?

"He said I shouldn't do anything strenuous for at least six weeks, so the muscle heals up properly. I don't know if I can make it six weeks, but I'll give it a good try."

"You've always been in great shape," Sonny said, "and a fast healer. Hopefully, you won't need a full six weeks. The way it's been the last couple months, we're likely to have another skip with a big paycheck waving over his head."

"That's why I don't think I'll make it six weeks."

"No... I'm just pulling your chain a little. We're going to make sure you're healed before you get wild and crazy."

"Yeah, and I do like the pampering from Vicki."

They finished their burgers, fries, and Pepsi's, and Dillon asked, "Any update on things?"

"Yeah, on a couple things. I spoke with Adele and she didn't get the commission for restoring the painting. Evidently the museum had an in-house person for that.

"Then I spoke with Lt. Helgeson and he said that Petrov and his cronies left Minnesota. He didn't know where they headed, but they're gone.

"And I spoke with several our clients, and all the skips we've brought in recently were convicted and are serving time somewhere.

"And... I guess that's it. That gets us all up to date."

"Well, it's been quite a couple months with a steady flow of skips and nice paydays," Dillon said. "I guess I won't mind a couple weeks off."

"Alright, I'd better get going," Sonny said, standing to leave. "You take care of yourself partner, hopefully everything will stay quiet for a few weeks. I'll talk to you tomorrow."

Dillon stood from his chair and walked around the table. With his good right arm, he gave Sonny a big hug and a slap on the back. "Thanks for everything partner."

"No thanks needed. You know I love ya."

Dillon looked at him for a moment, then said, "How did I ever get so lucky... to fall in with the best skip tracer there is for a partner?"

Then he held up his hand, and Sonny knew it meant, *No answer needed.*